I0603950

CYNTHIA HICKEY

Death By Baking

A Nosy Neighbor mystery, book 4

Cynthia Hickey

DEDICATION

To God. Thank you..

ACKNOWLEDGMENTS

To my husband, Tom, who gives up time with me on many weekends so I can finish the latest book. To my editor, Jan, who helps me make the book the best it can be, and to my readers who anxiously await the next cozy mystery. Thank you..

1

I, Stormi Nelson, NYT best-selling author, stared at my blank computer screen. Eight p.m. and I had yet to write a single word. I'd sent my assistant, Mary Ann Steele, home hours ago. Since she'd given up teaching in order to follow her dream of a job in the literary world, I needed to figure out the plot of my next romantic mystery, and fast.

Three months had passed since my venture into the world of gangsters and prostitutes. Before that, I'd battled a psycho fan who couldn't wait for me to write the next book. The first crime, the one that started me on the roller-coaster ride of solving a mystery, and then writing about it, had come strictly by accident. No one walked their dog with the intent of stumbling across a dead body, did they? None of these were my fault. I strictly chose to accept the opportunity to write the stories that fall into my lap.

Now, ordinary living seemed boring by comparison. I might as well take a stroll around the block on the pretense of watching the neighborhood. Since I'd started the neighborhood watch program over a year ago, I was still the prime member, along with my "little" neighbors next door, the Salazars.

"Come, Sadie." I clipped the leash to the collar of my Irish Wolfhound, the most chicken of any dog I'd ever met, and shuffled down the stairs and out into a mild spring evening.

My boyfriend, Matthew Steele, was out on another undercover assignment, leaving me to fill the long nights alone. Now that the basement apartment was converted into living space for my mother, the attic for my sister, and my teenage niece and nephew, Cherokee and Dakota out only God knew where, I found myself lonely again for the first time in a long time.

Once, I'd cherished my solitude. Now, that my family had moved in and I had a handsome man in my life, that very solitude wasn't so precious anymore.

I raised a hand to wave at the Olsons. Bill grinned and waved back—Mrs. Olson, I couldn't bring myself to call her Norma—simply glared. Someday, she might actually get it in her head that her roly-poly husband wasn't my type.

"Good evening, Rusty." My simple minded, but sweet-natured gardener glanced up from trimming the rose bushes. "It's kind of late to be pruning, isn't it?"

He nodded like one of those bobble heads people stick in their car windows. "Yep, but Rusty sees—"

"I know. Rusty sees things." He always said that, and sometimes the things he saw were things he shouldn't. "No peeking in people's windows, okay?"

"What about store windows?"

"That should be all right." I grinned and led Sadie across the street.

Hickory Street had a couple of

vacancies after the last three bouts of murders. Some of my neighbors actually blamed the downward turn on me. Said it had been a peaceful community until I moved in. I shrugged. First, they'd complained about me being a romance novelist, now they complained because I stuck my nose into whatever the current mystery, which always involved me somehow, and wrote another bestseller about it. I was careful to change people's names. Why should they be so concerned?

The thump thump of skateboard wheels over cracks in the sidewalk came up behind me. I glanced over my shoulder. "Hey, Dakota."

"Hey, Aunt Stormi." He hopped off his board and tucked it under his arm. "Where you going?"

"Neighborhood Watch work."

He laughed. "No one cares but you."

I shrugged. "They should. It also gives me exercise." The neighbors should care, especially with the happenings over the last year. Evil exists everywhere, even in a nice neighborhood like Oak

Meadows Estates, and most especially on Hickory Street where I lived. I seemed to bring trouble with me like a barge towing the iceberg that sunk the Titanic.

"A new old lady moved into the house on the corner," Dakota said, grinning. "She asked if I lived in the house where the red-haired woman fornicated on the front porch. I told her yes."

I whirled. "What?!"

Matt and I did not fornicate on the porch or anywhere else. We did indulge in some heavy make-out sessions occasionally, but I'd made a vow in high school to save myself until marriage. I still wore a purity ring on my pinky finger. Not that having a drop-dead gorgeous boyfriend helped the vow any, but still … I was a strong-willed woman. "She doesn't even know me."

"There she is." Dakota pointed.

I slapped his hand down. "Don't let on that we're talking about her." Too late. The short, round woman bustled toward us, her silver curls bouncing with each step.

"Are you that romance writer?" She planted pudgy fists on plump hips. "I was told by the realtor that this was a respectable neighborhood. Now, I find out we have a smut writer living here."

"Uh, that would be the other author in the community." I didn't write smut, but Sarah Thompson could make a porn star blush. "I write clean romantic mysteries with just enough sexual tension to keep you turning the page." I grinned and tugged Sadie past her.

She "hummphed" and marched away, her fuzzy house slippers slapping the pavement with each step. I probably shouldn't have provoked her, but I can't help myself when people confront me without cause.

Dakota tossed his skateboard onto the sidewalk, jumped on, and skated off with a wave. Sadie barked once and tugged against her leash as we passed Matt's and Mary Ann's house.

"Come sit for a spell," Mary Ann called. Not only was she my literary assistant, but my best friend. Between her and Mom, I never had to dig into a mystery alone. "Out looking for your next story?"

I sat on the porch swing next to her, looping Sadie's leash around my ankle. "No. But, I am at a loss as to what to write next."

"Make something up. Isn't that what fiction novelists do?" She set the swing into action with a nudge of her toe. "You've gotten spoiled."

I laughed. "Yes, I have. Let's brainstorm." I drummed my fingers on the arm of the swing and breathed deep of a nearby blooming honeysuckle bush. "We need a victim." The first one that came to mind was my new neighbor, and I didn't know her name. "Who's the new lady on the corner?"

"Betty Rogers. Watch out. She's called the police three times, and she's only been here a week."

"What does she call for?"

"Noises, dog poop, dog barking, you name it." Mary Ann shook her head. "She's going to drive my brother nuts once he gets home. Are you thinking of killing her off in a book?"

"Thought about it." I glanced toward her house. The curtains fell into place. "But there's no motive, other than being crotchety."

"She's a Nosy Nellie who saw something she shouldn't." Mary Ann waved at the old woman's house. "Who killed her?"

"Drug dealers?" No, that was done in my last book. "She witnessed a murder while out walking … does she have a dog?"

"Yes. Three yappy terriers."

Brainstorming a book was more fun with two people, even if the plot idea was too silly to use. "She was walking her dogs and noticed open curtains in a dark house. A light flickers. She goes to peek in—" My cell phone rang, playing the tune to Elvis's *Love Me Tender*.

I fished it from my pocket. "Matt!"

"Hey, beautiful. What are you doing?" His deep voice rumbled right into my heart.

"Plotting murder with your sister."

"On paper, I hope, and here I was going to talk dirty to you."

"Hush. She might hear." I turned my back to Mary Ann.

She laughed. "I'll fetch us some sodas while the two of you talk all lovey-dovey."

"I miss you," Matt and I said simultaneously.

"When are you coming home?" I slipped off my sandal and dangled Sadie's leash from my toes, which I had painted a bright Fuschia pink that morning.

"I'm not sure. This case is more complicated than I thought."

"I wish you would have stayed a small town detective. I worry about you."

"I'm fine. This isn't dangerous, but I do have to go. I love you."

"I love you, too." I sighed and hung up, working the leash back up to my ankle.

Mrs Rogers, clutching a leash that forked out to lead three small, wiry dogs marched past, her gaze straight ahead of her. Sadie yelped and tore off the porch, dragging me from the swing.

I shrieked and landed with a thump

on my backside, knocking the breath from my lungs. Oh, that hurt.

Three dogs yipped, one giant wolfhound bounded in circles, and I lay on the floor of the porch like a beached fish. I tried to wheeze out Sadie's name to call her back, but nothing escaped. My mouth opened and closed.

"Get this beast off my babies!" Mrs. Rogers danced around as her three dogs wrapped her in the leash.

I pushed to my knees, then wrapped my arms around the porch railing as Mary Ann exited the house. I motioned toward the fiasco on the sidewalk.

She set the drinks on a small wooden table and dashed down the steps. "I'm so sorry, Mrs. Rogers."

"I'm calling the police to have that monster put down. It's a menace."

No. Not my big lovable baby. Still doubled over, I made my way down the stairs and to the sidewalk. "I'm so sorry. She only wants to play."

Mrs. Rogers glared. "I should have known the dog was yours."

I finally caught my breath enough to

straighten. "She is very tame and sweet. She would not have hurt your dogs, except to maybe love them to death."

Her eyes narrowed. "Now, you're threatening my puppies with death?"

"No, I was only—"

"Let's go, my darlings." She tugged on the leash, rather roughly in my opinion, and dragged the little dogs across the street.

Mary Ann met my startled gaze. "She'll have the cops here in ten minutes. Matt is going to kill both of us."

I wrapped Sadie's leash around my wrist. "Maybe she *will* be the next victim in my book." Killing off people, on paper anyway, was a great stress reliever. "I'm going home. My backside hurts. When Officer Jones arrives, send him to my house. Angela will be thrilled." It didn't matter to my somewhat seductively dressed sister that the officer was dating the 9-1-1 operator. She still preened like a peacock whenever he came around.

"Okay. See you tomorrow."

I made my way, limping, to the Victorian home that I'd purchased a year and a half ago, still getting pleasure from the sight of the turrets and wraparound porches. After sending Sadie inside, I sat in a padded rocking chair and waited for the police. While I waited, I plotted further in getting revenge on one nasty old lady, on paper, of course.

Fifteen minutes later, Wayne Jones, the second best looking officer on the small police force of Oak Meadows, stopped in front of the house. Before he could get out of his car, Mom roared into the driveway, flinging gravel from the tires of her beat up minivan.

She thrust open her door and sprinted for the house, her hired help, Greta, at her heels. "Get rid of him," Mom hissed, motioning toward Officer Jones. "We've another murder to solve."

2

"Explain yourself, Mrs Nelson." Officer Jones narrowed dark eyes. The man knew not to get too excited about anything Mom said until he had more information. She often made too much of something small, and too little of something big. I had a feeling this was something big.

Mom sighed, clearly wanting to keep the information to herself. I'd tried, to no avail, to make her realize that the cops were the real experts in crime solving. Not us. We should consider it more of a … hobby.

"There's a dead man with his head stuck in my chocolate batter."

Officer Jones's eyebrows raised. "Excuse me?"

"Dead, drowned, something." She waved a hand. "At the bakery. In my batter."

He turned and raced to his squad car as Mom, Greta, and I made a dash for the minivan. Ignoring my bruised behind, I plopped into the front passenger seat and clasped the seat belt across me. "Don't let him get there too far ahead of us. He'll rope it all off, and we won't be able to see a thing."

Mom tapped her forefinger against her temple. "I already thought of that. The good Lord didn't give me a brain for nothing. I left the back door unlocked."

Oh, good. Because no self-respecting law enforcement officer would think to check the back door. I rolled my eyes and silently urged Mom to drive faster. We had to get inside the shop before Officer Jones locked the place up.

Adrenaline coursed through me. I'd found the plot of my next book without even trying. It was a gift the way I stumbled onto these things. I chose to think that way rather than thinking of it as a curse.

Mom jerked the wheel, sending us rocketing down the alley. We screeched to a halt at the bakery's back door and tumbled out of the van like upended blocks. We barreled through the door the same time Officer Jones rushed in the front.

"You belong in NASCAR, Mrs. Nelson," he said, shaking his head. "I ought to give you a ticket for speeding. Just stay out of my way, please."

"We will." I moved to where a man in a business suit bent over a vat of chocolate. If not for the fact he was so far in that his feet didn't reach the floor, I would have thought he merely searched for something. "Why so much chocolate?"

"We have a huge order for volcano cakes." Mom bent over and peered into the vat. "I don't recognize this man. Maybe, if I could see his face."

"Step back, please." Officer Jones pushed between her and the victim. He shoved his hand into the man's pocket and withdrew a wallet. "It's Jim Worthington."

"The bookstore owner?" I slumped against the worktable. I'd always liked the friendly older gentleman. He always greeted me with a smile and a nudge toward the shelf of new releases. "Why would anyone want to kill him?"

"We don't know that his death wasn't an accident," Officer Jones stated.

"You think he just happened to fall into a vat of baking chocolate?" I crossed my arms. "Not likely. What was he doing here after hours?" What was Mom doing here so late?

"We left to head to the grocery store for more flour," Mom said. "We were gone more than an hour, and returned to find him like …this. Oh, the poor man."

"If I was going to drown," Greta said, "there's no better way than with chocolate."

"Ladies, please." Officer Jones ushered us to the front of the store. "Stay here and don't let anyone in but the authorities. Definitely no press."

"They're already here." I stared out the window as Nancy Rhino, I meant Rhinehart, stepped from her silver Volvo and made her way to the door.

She tapped on the glass with a long,

manicured, scarlet nail. "Let me in."

I shook my head. "Police orders."

"Come on, Stormi. We went to high school together."

It wasn't my fault she followed me from Little Rock to Oak Meadows. We hadn't been best friends then, and we definitely weren't now. Not after she left a scathing review of one of my earlier books. She could've derailed my entire writing career. Where would I be now if she had?

"You're impossible, Red!"

"No more than you, Rhino!" We'd reverted to the childishness of school in a matter of minutes.

She cupped her hands around her eyes and plastered her face to the window, leaving a smudge of makeup on the clean glass. "Is that Mr. Worthington?"

"No comment."

"Is he dead?"

"No comment!" I crossed my arms and glared.

"Ugh!" She stomped away and leaned against her car.

She must have spotted Officer Jones's squad car. There was no other way she could have found out so quickly that there was a body in the bakery.

Within ten minutes, quite a crowd had gathered in front of the store. Mom filled a tray with finger cookies and stepped outside, passing them around. "Nothing like free advertising," she said upon reentering the store.

I frowned. "That's gross. We have a dead man in the back and you're marketing?"

"I believe in taking advantage of opportunities." She slid the tray under the counter. "While I feel bad for the man, I didn't kill him. Why should business have to suffer?"

"It's going to suffer for a while," Greta said. "They'll close us down until they process the area and the Medical Examiner releases the body."

"But the anniversary order!"

I sighed. She'd take over my kitchen again, just when I had a weekend of cooking planned. Filling my freezer with frozen casseroles was my way of relaxing. Now, I'd have to find time in-between Mom's baking.

"I'm asking the three of you to leave." Officer Jones joined them. "Once the CSI team arrives from Little Rock, this place will be inaccessible for at least three days. Take what you need now and go home. Don't leave town."

Mom groaned and grabbed a thick notebook from under the counter. "We'll have to get more chocolate from the warehouse store. There's no time to order from our regular supplier. Oh, what am I going to do?"

Greta patted her shoulder. "We'll make do. No one will know the chocolate is a substitute. I'll be over first thing in the morning so we can replenish our supplies."

When had my normally caring mother grown so selfish? Had my purchasing the store for her turned her into a self-absorbed monster?

I cast one more glance at the crowd through the window. Was the killer watching? They always returned to the scene of the crime on television shows.

Could it be one of the two men in suits leaning against the coffee shop wall? Or was it one of the ordinary looking citizens who looked as if they hadn't seen anything more interesting in their lives?

Either way, I'd give my laptop if the killer wasn't one of them, watching and gloating as Officer Jones stood guard over Mr. Worthington's body. I put a hand over my heart, feeling a physical ache at the nice man's untimely death, and pulled the string overhead to close the blinds. Show's over, folks.

I followed Mom and Greta to the van at a more sedate pace than we'd entered the store. They were already chattering like birds about the new crime to solve. While I'd thought it a good thing at first, now sadness filled me. Did someone have to die for me to have a new story idea? Mary Ann was right. I needed to start planning my plots from nothing, like other fiction writers. Making my money off the misfortune of others was starting to give me a sick feeling in the pit of my stomach.

As soon as we got home, I dialed my

agent from the phone in my office and left a message for her to call me in the morning. It wouldn't hurt for me to get her professional opinion on what she thought my readers would like.

Once I'd done that, I joined Mom and Greta in the kitchen. Mom had a sketchpad in front of her.

"I'm not sure I want to get involved in this," I said, sitting down. "It doesn't seem right to continue writing about the death of others."

"We have to get involved." Mom glanced up from the paper. "We're suspects. Didn't you hear Officer Jones tell us not to leave town? That means we're the primary suspects."

"You watch too much television."

"She does own the store, Stormi," Greta said. "That makes her a suspect, and you, too. If the authorities drag their feet, we could be working out of your kitchen for quite a while. We need to get to the bottom of this and get back to work."

"Can't we at least give it a day or two? Or at least until Mr. Worthington is buried?"

"You're really shook up about this, aren't you?" Mom laid a hand over mine. "What's wrong? Did you know him well?"

"No, but I'm a bestselling author because people are dying!" I lay my head on my folded arms and cried. "I feel like a horrible person."

"The first time was an accident. The second time you were forced into a story by a weirdo. The third time … well, you were helping your sister."

I glanced up. "This time? There is no reason."

"I see your predicament." Greta crossed her arms. "We'll solve this crime because we're addicted, and you stick to fiction. Unless you feel like taking a break and want to help us. You know you love solving puzzles as much as we do."

True. There was a certain lure to racing against the police to catch a murderer. Of course, there was a certain element of danger, too, that was as addictive as any drug. The best thing I could compare it to was typing The End on a story I knew my readers would devour. I was hooked on solving mysteries, whether on paper or in real life.

"Okay." I nodded and wiped my face on my sleeve. "I'll help you find Mr. Worthington's killer, but I won't write about it."

"I knew you'd come around." Mom gave my hand another pat, then turned to the paper in front of her. "What possible motive would anyone have to kill a bookstore owner?"

"I think it's too early to write down anything," I said. "You need more information. We don't even know for sure how he was killed. We'll have Angela try to find that out at work." Since my sister was the receptionist for the local police department, her sharp ears often heard things the rest of us weren't privy to.

"I'll do it." Angela sashayed into the kitchen, wearing baby doll pajamas better worn on a teenage girl in the 1950s. "Y'all didn't know I was standing there listening. That's how good I am at spying. But …" She held up a finger. "If you get me killed, I'll come back to haunt you. I swear."

"What in heaven's name are you wearing?" Mom paled. "Do you know how old you are?"

Angela ran her hands over her pajamas. "What's wrong with them? They look innocent and sweet, right? I'm hoping Officer Wayne Jones will come back by to question you some more. I'll act all embarrassed and dash upstairs."

"Flashing just a bit of your behind." I shoved back my chair. "I'm going to bed. I doubt we'll have any visitors tonight." Mom had done something wrong raising my little sister. Two children with different fathers, and dressing like she was fifteen.

I eyed my sensible blue Capris and navy tank top. While I'd updated my wardrobe upon dating Matt, compared to Angela, I was an old woman at the age of twenty-eight. Oh, well. At least I didn't have people other than Mrs. Olson or Mrs. Rogers questioning my morals.

I threw myself across the bed and

stared at the ceiling. The street light outside cast the room in shadows. I glanced at the clock and saw it was almost eleven p.m. My night had filled up after all. I didn't think I'd whine about being bored again. Nothing good came of it.

3

"Good morning!" Mary Ann plopped into the office chair at the second desk I'd purchased once we decided she would be my literary assistant. "I heard you had quite the night."

"How did you hear that?" I spun in my chair and noticed her empty hands. "Where's my coffee?"

"Well," she tilted her head. "I have my sources, and since the coffee shop is across the street from the bookstore, I thought you might like to go with me and do a bit of snooping." She dangled a key. "I used to work for Mr. Worthington in high school. I doubt he changed the locks on the store in all these years. People in this town aren't much for change."

"I've decided I'm not going to profit anymore from people's misfortune."

"Don't you want to know how he died? You don't have to write about it. We'll work more on the story about killing off Mrs. Rogers. This is something we can do to keep the creative juices flowing. Please?"

The lure of the mystery stuck in the corner of my mouth and tugged me toward the door. I grabbed my purse. "Let's go. I can't work without my coffee."

I got in the passenger side of Mary Ann's Volkswagen Beetle, tossed a wave to nosy Mrs. Rogers, who peered through her curtains, and settled back for the short drive to Main Street. Coffee and snooping, the perfect way to start the day.

Who was I kidding? Heartache and compassion or not, I'd be writing about the latest fiasco in Oak Meadows. I could mourn the loss of Mr. Worthington and write, couldn't I? I had to give my readers what they wanted.

"Does Mr. Worthington have any family?"

"He's married." Mary Ann parked in front of Delicious Aroma. "His wife is a sweetheart. A bit on the shy side and stays home a lot, but I'm sure she'll see us."

"I'd like to get her permission before digging any further into her husband's death."

She nodded and cut the ignition. "Then, we'll go there next. That's a wonderful idea."

My cell phone rang. Caller ID said it was my agent. "Do you mind?" I asked Mary Ann. "You know what I like."

"Sure." She bounded from the car and into the store.

"Hey, Elizabeth."

"You called?"

I explained my dilemma. "Today I've decided to wait until I talk to the victim's wife before pursuing the story."

"That's a good idea." She remained silent for a moment. "Stormi, you don't have to put yourself in danger or compromise your principles for a story. You're a talented writer. You have a hundred stories locked in that head of yours. Your readers won't care where the story comes from. They just want the next one.”

"Thank you.” A weight lifted off my shoulders. If Mrs. Worthington has any qualms at all about me digging into her husband's death, and possibly writing about it, I'll stop.

"So?” Mary Ann handed me my drink as I hung up.

"If Mrs. Worthington is fine with it, it's a go.” Mom and Greta would be tickled pink.

We drove fifteen minutes out of town and pulled up to a modest bungalow complete with white picket fence and flowers. Two rocking chairs adorned the front porch. A bird bath and hummingbird feeder sat under an ancient magnolia tree. It was the cutest house I'd ever seen; something out of a fairytale.

A tiny woman emerged from around the corner of the house before we had gotten out of the car. She fairly skipped, swinging a basket of fresh cut blooms on her arms. She hummed a snappy tune I didn't recognize. Once she spotted us, she froze. If this was Mrs. Worthington, she looked nothing like a grieving widow.

I exchanged a surprised look with Mary Ann and approached the house. "Mrs. Worthington?"

She nodded.

"I'm Stormi Nelson, and this is my assistant, Mary Ann Steele." I held out my hand. "Our condolences on the death of your husband."

She wiped her hand on her dress and returned my shake. "Thank you. It's a … terrible thing. Please, come in." She led the way into a house as quaint inside as out.

Doilies covered the arms of chairs and the sofa. A quilted table runner adorned the kitchen table, and over it all hung the scent of baking cookies.

"I used to work for your husband," Mary Ann said, taking a seat at the table.

"I remember. You always were a sweet little thing." Mrs. Worthington busied herself at the counter, taking glasses from the cupboard. "I've cookies and fresh-squeezed lemonade. Jim always wanted some around. I guess it will take a while to break the habit."

"Mrs. Worthington?" I sat and folded my arms on the table. "I'd like to dig into how your husband died and write a story about it. Are you opposed to that?"

She stiffened, then her shoulders slumped as she faced us. "Not one iota. But you make sure you get your facts straight. You hear me? None of this false information about what a wonderful, caring, sweetheart he was. Jim Worthington was none of that." She slammed her hand on the table. "None!"

She took a deep breath and smiled. "But, I'm not one to speak ill of the dead. You'll have to get your information from someone else. Lemonade?"

"Oh, uh," Mary Ann glanced at me with wide eyes.

I stood. "No, I'm afraid we have a very busy day ahead of us. Again, we're sorry for your loss, and if there is anything I can do for you, please don't hesitate to call me." I scribbled my cell phone number on a napkin, forced a smile, and dashed out the door as if the hounds of hell were on my heels.

Mary Ann must have been as spooked

as I was. She peeled rubber from the driveway and headed back to town in record time. She pulled into the alley behind the bookstore. "We forgot to get permission."

"I'm not going back there to ask." I shoved my door open and headed for the back door of the shop, holding my hand out for the key.

"I guess she kind of said we could. I mean, she said we could investigate." Mary Ann dropped the key into my palm and stepped back, glancing up and down the alley as if we were on the verge of being discovered doing something illegal. We weren't, were we?

The key slid into a well-oiled lock and within seconds, Mary Ann and I were safe from prying eyes and in the dim recesses of the town's one and only bookstore. I loved the smell of paper and ink. I took a deep breath.

Mary Ann flipped on the light, revealing a workspace covered with boxes of books. "Who is going to run this store now? Look at all these. It will be a shame if they're tossed."

"Maybe Mrs. Worthington will take over the store once she's done grieving." Ha! The woman hadn't shown an ounce of grief. I'd say she was rather happy over her husband's death.

"What are we looking for?" Mary Ann opened a file cabinet.

"Anything that might explain why he was killed." Hopefully, my sister was finding some information at the police station. Mainly, cause of death.

"What are you doing?"

Mary Ann and I screamed and plastered ourselves across the wall as Mom and Greta barged through the back door. We should have locked it.

"Not funny." My heart beat so fast, it was a wonder no one could hear it. "Mrs. Worthington said it was all right if we investigated. We thought we'd start here." I narrowed my eyes. "Why are the two of you here?"

"We had the same idea." Mom grinned. "It was a nice surprise to find the door unlocked. Greta thought we might have to break in."

For an ex-police officer, Mom's

sidekick walked a thin line. "The two of you are going to be the death of me. Go look for clues," I ordered.

Mom had no sooner opened the office door to the main room of the store, before the bell jingled over the glass doors in front. We left the office door cracked, turned off the light, and hunkered down to eavesdrop and wait.

"Who is it?" Mom hissed.

"I don't know." I put a finger to my lips.

"What do they want?"

"I don't know. Hush." Seriously.

"I doubt the widow will resume business," a man said. "We should be able to purchase this place for a song."

"What about the other stores along this street?" another man asked.

"You let me worry about that."

"Gentlemen, if you'd like to take a deeper look, I'm sure you'll find the place more than satisfactory for your purposes."

I knew that third voice. It belonged to Jane Weston of Weston Realty. She sure wasn't wasting any time selling off Mr.

Worthington's pride and joy. First his wife, now Jane. Did no one mourn his passing?. What kind of man had he been? It was becoming quite obvious that the kindly gentleman I once knew was possibly a façade.

"I think we're done here," man number one said. "We plan on gutting the space, anyway."

"That will be a pity," Jane said. "These shops are all part of our historical society. We pride ourselves in keeping Main Street looking much as it had when the town was founded. In order to make major changes, you'll have to get committee approval."

"I'm sure the store owners will be more than compensated."

The bell jingled again, signaling they'd left. We unfolded ourselves from behind the work counter.

"I don't like the sound of that," Mom said. "It sounds like some strangers are wanting to buy up Main Street. Do you think that's why Mr. Worthington was killed and dumped in my chocolate? As a way of running me off? Kill him, scare me, and take care of two at once?"

"Have you been approached about selling?" I faced her.

"No."

"Then there must be another reason." Killing for property was one of the oldest tactics in the book. But then, how many reasons were there for killing? It seemed most of the time to come down to fame or money. "Let's go before someone finds us."

We filed out the back door and ran smack dab into Officer Jones. He exhaled sharply. "Explain yourselves."

"Now, Wayne." I held up a hand. "Don't get upset. Mrs. Worthington gave us permission to investigate her husband's death."

"She did?" Mom glanced at me.

He shook his head. "You know better than to interfere. Hasn't Steele taught you anything?"

Well, yeah, Matt and I had gone over plenty of times the reasons why I shouldn't butt my nose into the police's business, but I couldn't help myself. "We promise to stay out of your way and to share any information we find."

"I'm not your boyfriend, Stormi. I will arrest you if you interfere."

"Then, we'll stay out of your way." I ushered the group into their vehicles and whispered for everyone to congregate at my house. I had a baked spaghetti dish I'd heat up while we compared notes.

"I mean it!" Officer Jones yelled after us as we backed from the alley.

I tossed him a wave out the window. Maybe he should date my sister. She might loosen him up a bit. No one who hung around our family long enough could resist our charm. He'd be spilling his guts within days.

Not that Matt told me everything I wanted to know about the crimes around town, but I managed to get enough out of him to stay one step ahead of the killer. This time, Matt was out of town. Who was going to keep me alive?

4

"It's too early for spaghetti," Mom said when I pulled a casserole dish from the freezer.

"It's for lunch. It'll take a while to thaw." I rolled my eyes, something I seemed to be doing a lot lately, and opened the kitchen window to allow a breeze to circulate. I grabbed a notepad and pencil and sat at the table. "We now know that Mrs. Worthington didn't care much for her husband, that he wasn't a nice guy, at least in her eyes, and that someone wants to buy the businesses on Main Street." I scribbled the notes on the notepad.

"Of course she isn't distraught," Mom said. "I didn't want to say anything yesterday, but Jim Worthington was nothing more than a wife beater. A brilliant seller of books, but not a nice man in his personal life."

"Do you think she killed him?" I still wanted to know how the man got into Mom's store, and why.

"That tiny thing?" Mom shook her head. "It took some force to shove his head far enough into the chocolate that his feet didn't touch the floor."

True. I tapped the pencil eraser against my lips. "We still don't know how he died."

"Yes, we do." Mary Ann held up her hand. "He died with blunt force trauma to the head and was dead before being put into the vat." She grinned. "No chocolate in his lungs."

"Was he killed in the store?" Greta leaned forward.

Mary Ann punched buttons on her phone. Seconds later, a ding announced a text. "No."

"Who are you texting?" I sipped my frozen mocha drink, that after the visit with Mrs. Worthington, wasn't so frozen.

"My source." Her cheeks darkened.

"Who is he?" I smiled around my straw. "I seem to recall Matt saying something about a new rookie down at the station. He must be cute for you to turn so red."

"He's all right." She kept her head down. "Are you going to grill me or find out what happened to Mr. Worthington?"

"I can do both." I reached over and tossed my empty cup in the garbage. "I'm going to have to make a trip to the station and meet this new guy."

Mom cleared her throat. "I have a confession to make."

We quieted.

"Jim and I did not exactly get along."

"Define exactly," I said.

She huffed, tearing a napkin into tiny pieces. "We've had several arguments about my bakery. He said people came into his store to smell books, not cakes. He approached me several times about expanding and wanted to buy me out."

"Did you tell Officer Jones this?"

"No. I'm afraid if they knew, then they would have even more reason to suspect me."

"Mom! You can't keep information like that from the police. It only makes you look guiltier."

She shrugged. "I suppose I can tell them when we go in today to give our statements."

"We're supposed to go in?"

"Officer Jones told us last night to come in today. You must have been so busy arguing with that news reporter that you didn't hear him."

Criminy. Of course, we'd have to give a statement. "Let's go. I'm sure he expected us this morning." I grabbed my purse, flipped the notepad over, and stormed out the front door. If I did eventually get arrested, it would be because of something my mother did, or didn't do. Not on my own merits.

I was already buckled into the van by the time the others came out. "I'm heading home for a while," Mary Ann said through the vehicle window. "I still have labels to type up for your next mailing. Let me know if you find out anything interesting."

"Like if we're going to jail?" I glared

at Mom. "We should have gone first thing this morning."

"Like you're one to talk. I remember when Matthew had to hunt you up to get your statement. Besides, the bakery belongs to me. You have nothing to do with this."

"I learned my lesson, and my name is on the title!"

"Good for you." She turned the key in the ignition and put the van in reverse. "Watch your feet, Mary Ann. We'll call you when it's time for lunch." Mom drove to the station in stony silence.

I probably shouldn't have barked at her, but with Matt gone, I tended to go overboard in trying to do the right thing. When he wasn't away on assignment, I felt as if the other officers gave me a bit of leeway. They would rather send Matt to deal with me, than have to do it themselves.

We pulled in front of the station as Officer Jones was coming out. He shook his head and turned to go back inside. I glared at Mom. "I bet he was coming to get us."

"Stop being such a brat." She cut the engine. "We're here now."

"I'm sorry." I stopped her from exiting the van. "I'm scared, Mom. This isn't the same as tripping over a body in the dark or receiving threatening emails. This is close to home. I don't want to go to jail while Matt is gone."

"We're not going to jail." She patted my hand and led the way into the station.

Angela glanced up from the receptionist desk. "Run," she hissed.

"What?" I swallowed against the sudden boulder in my throat.

"Wayne was on his way to see you and Mom. You should have been here first thing this morning. He's steaming." She grabbed a coffee mug from her desk. "First door on the right. I'll bring coffee, uh, later."

Liar. She was going to hide.

She lowered her voice. "He called Matt."

The blood drained from my head to my feet. I slipped my hand into the pocket of my denim shorts, tempted to push the off button.

Mom and Greta marched into the conference room, leaving me to shuffle behind them. Officer Jones sat at the end of a rectangular table and stared, unblinking, like an owl.

"Close the door," he said.

I pulled the door closed, envisioning the bars of a cell clanging shut behind me. Taking a deep breath, I leaned my forehead against the small glass window set in the door panel.

"Stop being so dramatic," Officer Jones said. "Sit down. It's your mother that is in trouble."

"I guess you found out." Mom sighed and set her giant purse on the table.

"Found out what, Mrs. Nelson?"

Everything in me wanted to tell Mom to be quiet. Couldn't she tell she was being led into confessing something? I slumped into a chair.

"That Jim and I had a few altercations." She leaned on the table. "But that doesn't mean I killed him."

"Do you recognize this?" He set a large plastic bag between them. Inside was a wooden, French-style rolling pin.

"We'll get back to the altercation you mentioned."

"That's mine." Mom reached for it. "Why do you have it?"

"This was the murder weapon, Mrs. Nelson." He placed it back out of sight. "When was the last time you saw it?"

"Yesterday afternoon." Mom paled. "I use it all the time."

"Did you use it to kill Jim Worthington?"

"No! We argued over the fact he could smell my baking in his bookstore, but we never got physical."

"Maybe you killed him to get him off your back?"

She shook her head vehemently. "I did that just fine by using my words." She stared at her hands. "Am I under arrest?"

"No, but you're our main suspect. I'm releasing you under Greta's supervision." He narrowed his eyes. "As a former police officer, I trust her to keep you in line."

I bit back a snort. Of the three of us, I was by far the most responsible, and that wasn't saying a lot. "We'll make sure she doesn't go anywhere."

He cocked his head. "Stay out of it, Stormi."

Hey, that was Matt's line. "Mrs. Worthington asked us to investigate her husband's death. I intend to do just that." I gave him a thin-lipped smile. "I already promised to share any information we found."

"Have you discovered anything?" He crossed his arms.

"Did you know there are men interested in buying all the shops on Main Street?"

He laughed. "Old news, Stormi. There is always someone out to buy prime real estate."

"But someone is actively trying to do so."

"We're finished here. I'll be in touch." He pushed to his feet and stormed from the room, leaving the three of us to stare dumbfounded at each other.

"Let's get out of here while I'm still a free woman." Mom grabbed her purse and pushed past my seat to get out. She didn't stop until she stood on the top step of the station. Taking deep breaths, she closed her eyes. "Fresh air never smelled sweeter."

I rolled my eyes, then froze as *Love Me Tender* erupted from my pocket. Forcing myself to sound chipper, I pressed the answer button. "Hey, sweetheart."

"Uh huh. What's going on now, Stormi?"

Okay, straight to the point. "Mom is under suspicion for killing the bookstore owner."

"Tell me something I don't know. Like, why are you getting involved?"

I leaned against the warm brick of the building. "I can't not get involved. Not now, when Mom's been accused of murder. Besides, the widow gave me permission. When are you coming home? You can help us."

"Soon." He sighed. "Baby, you know how your hobby scares me."

I practically melted every time he called me baby. "I'm being careful. We don't even have a bonafide suspect yet."

"I hate when you talk like that. Look, sweetheart, I've got to go. Please, move slow until I get home."

"I have to keep my mother out of jail."

"Who would have ever thought I'd care for a woman who had reason to say those words? I love you. Gotta go." Click.

"I love you, too," I whispered to a silent phone, before joining Mom and Greta in the van. While we headed home, I texted Mary Ann to let her know we were on our way.

She met us at the front door. "Mrs. Worthington has disappeared."

"What?!" I shoved open the van door. "Get in."

She slid into the back.

"How do you know?"

"I tried to call her. When she didn't answer, I called her neighbor. They said they saw her tossing things into the back of her Toyota before she sped away."

"Turn right up here, Mom." If that wasn't the actions of a guilty person, I didn't know what was. Petite or not, I was putting my money on the widow as Jim's killer.

Sure enough, no Toyota sat in front of the cute little cottage. "The front door is still open," I said, emerging from the car.

I climbed the three steps and pushed the door open. The house looked exactly as it had that morning. If Mrs. Worthington was leaving, she wasn't taking a lot with her.

"Come out." Mary Ann grabbed my arm and yanked me back out the door. "She's back."

The four of us oozed guilt as Mrs. Worthington rushed toward us. I fidgeted with my hands in my pockets. The last thing we needed was for her to call the police because we were trespassing.

"What now?" She brushed past us and into the house. "Y'all sure don't believe in letting a woman grieve in peace, do you?"

"Are you grieving?" I raised my eyebrows. "Not that it's any of my business, but you seem as far from the grieving widow as is possible."

"You're right. It's none of your

business." She whipped open a closet and started tossing coats into a box. "What I do is not your concern. I'm going to sell that store for a high price and live in comfort for the rest of my life."

"What are you packing?"

She straightened and grinned. "All my dear husband's belongings. I can't bear the sight of them. His death is my freedom."

5

Stunned, shocked, horrified, all of the above, our little foursome trooped out to the van and left the widow to her glee. I clicked on my seatbelt and stared out the window at the cottage.

Mrs. Worthington skipped outside with a full box, placed it in the trunk of her car, and hopped back inside the house. How awful to lose your spouse and be so happy about it. I made a mental note to return the next day and question the neighbors about the relationship between the bookstore owner and his happy little wife.

Mom drove us home where I popped the thawed spaghetti casserole into the oven. "This mystery is a bit … confusing," I said. "Usually, we have some kind of clue by the second day. All

I can come up with is the widow did it in the kitchen with the rolling pin."

"Not funny." Mom glared. Being a widow who spent a lot of time in the kitchen with baking utensils, she obviously didn't find my reference funny.

"Maybe you should stick with killing off Mrs. Rogers," Mary Ann said.

A crash sounded outside the kitchen window. I parted the curtains and glanced out. Sadie ran from the window to the rear of the house and back again, a big doggy grin on her face. Under the window, several empty flower pots were scattered across the lawn. Silly dog. Always getting into something.

"Oh, that plot is definitely on the burner." I opened the fridge, noted we had plenty of sweet tea made, and then grabbed the trusty notepad. "What is y'all's gut reaction to Mrs. Worthington?"

"If she wasn't so small," Mom said, "I would say she did it."

"Maybe she had someone else do it." Mary Ann glanced around the table. "If she was unhappy in her marriage, perhaps she had a boyfriend. Someone who would want to share in her fortune once her husband was gone."

"That makes perfect sense." I stabbed the pencil into the air for emphasis. "Her boyfriend killed him. Very cliché, but who am I to judge? I just can't shake the idea that she had something to do with Jim's death."

Mary Ann got up and moved to the window. She made a shushing motion with her hand.

"What?" Mom frowned.

"Shh. I think someone has been listening. There's scuff marks in the flower bed." She sighed. "If so, they're gone now. Stormi, why can't you have a dog worth something?"

"She is worth something. She's a great big love bug." I glared.

"She's worthless as a guard dog." Mary Ann resumed her seat. "It was probably just Rusty."

I didn't think he would duck out of sight if discovered, since he didn't see anything wrong with peeping in windows, but there was always a first time. I pointed everyone's attention back to the paper. "Okay, let's assume it isn't Mrs. Worthington. We also have the unidentified voices we heard in the bookstore." I jotted a note to make an appointment to talk to Jane Weston. Maybe if I pretended to be interested in buying or selling another property, I could get her to open up about the business on Main Street.

I made a column on the paper listed "Things to Do". So far, I had talk to Mrs. Worthington's neighbors, and make an appointment with Jane Weston. I tapped the eraser against my teeth and stared at three sets of eyes focused on me.

"What else?" I asked.

"Find out about a boyfriend," Mary Ann said.

"Find out how Jim got in my bakery," Mom stated.

Greta clapped her hands once together, the sound loud in the kitchen. "Find out who the men in the bookstore are."

I nodded. "This gives me a good place to start."

"What do you want us to do? We can't do much," Mom said, "since we have baking to do, but we could maybe set up a meeting with investors about the possibility of selling the store."

I shook my head. "Not without me there. That could be very dangerous." The timer on the stove alerted us to the fact lunch was ready. "Since I'm co-owner of the store, it would make sense for me to be there."

I pulled plates from the overhead cabinet and stacked them on the counter before pulling the casserole from the oven. Baked cheese and tomato greeted me. I sniffed deeply, wishing I had thought to make fresh garlic bread. No problem. We had frozen slices in the freezer.

"Do y'all think we've ruined any chance of asking Mrs. Worthington about who is buying the bookstore?" I covered the casserole with tin foil and pulled the bread from the freezer, sliding the foiled package into the oven. "I mean, the last time we were there was clearly for nothing more than snooping."

"You could always go on the pretense of pretending we're going to sell and want the best price." Mom poured us each a glass of tea. "What's the worst she can do? Run you off her property? Call the cops? We've been there, done that. Nothing new."

The doorbell rang, pulling me away from lunch preparations. "Watch the bread," I told Mom. Wiping my hands on a dishcloth, I moved to the front door and peered out the window.

Ugh. Officer Jones stood on the porch, looking very unhappy.

I opened the door. "Yes, sir?"

"May I come in?" No smile, no niceties, just business. This couldn't be good news.

I sighed and stepped back. "Please do. We're in the kitchen having lunch. You're welcome to join us."

"No, thanks. This won't take long." He followed me into the kitchen where Mom was cutting and serving the casserole. "Ladies." He took a deep breath. "Have you been discussing ways to kill Mrs. Rogers?"

So, that's who was listening at the window. "It's a plot for one of my books. We aren't murderers, Wayne. You know that." I crossed my arms. "Can't I have her arrested for trespassing and eavesdropping on private property?" That's what she got for being so sneaky.

"Do you want me to arrest her? She's an old woman." He looked at me as if I was a bad person for saying such a thing and using his first name.

"At least talk to her and tell her to stay off my property. Eavesdroppers rarely hear anything good."

"I can't wait until Matt returns." He breathed sharply through his nose. "You're too much work." He turned and stormed from the house, muttering something about talking to Mrs. Rogers.

I couldn't wait until Matt returned either. At least when he scolded me, he followed up with a hug and a kiss. Wayne Jones didn't even bother with a smile.

I ate in silence, my mind going over what little we knew about Jim's murder and what I needed to do to find out more.

Without some kind of schedule, I'd get very little actual work done on my writing. "Mary Ann, as my assistant, we're going to snoop before lunch and do writing related things after lunch. It might take longer to solve this crime, but I do have to make a living."

"You need to delegate," Mom said. "We can cover a lot more ground if you do."

This must be how Matt feels when I venture out on my own. The thought of Mom questioning potential murderers chilled my blood. I wanted my family as far away from this new "hobby" of mine as possible. Difficult, since Mom enjoyed the investigating as much as I did.

"I know that look," she said. "You can't do this alone. Either you don't do it at all, or we all help."

Sometimes I felt badgered into the crime-solving business. All to sell a book? Was it worth it? The danger, the excitement, the time away from my laptop? Yes. I loved it.

"Okay." I assigned her the task of finding out who the investors were, but not to actually meet with them until I could be there. Mary Ann and I would visit Mrs. Worthington and her neighbors. Maybe one of them would give us something to go on as to where Jim was actually killed. The main stipulation Matt had put on my investigating was that I not do it alone.

"Smells good." Angela moseyed into the kitchen and plucked a piece of baked cheese off Mom's plate. "I've got news," she sang. "Can't stay long. I'm on my lunch break, but I thought you might be interested in knowing that there was blood splatter found in the alley outside the bakery. Forensics are checking to see whether it's a match to Jim or not. We won't know anything for a few weeks."

"That's wonderful!" I jumped up and almost hugged her, stopping only when her lip started to curl. "Now we know where he was killed."

"Thank you." She ate a forkful of Mom's lunch. "I wanted to tell you in person rather than over the phone. Too many ears at the station. Bye." With a wave of her fingers, she was gone.

Maybe I didn't give my sister enough credit. She had just come through in a big way. I wrote down alley next to the question of where Jim was killed.

Mom twisted her mouth, deep in thought, and twirled her fork in her spaghetti.

"What's bothering you, Mom?"

"If Jim was killed in the alley, then how did the killer get my rolling pin?"

Excellent question. "Who wants to take a ride?"

We raced from the house like a bunch of puppies heading for the feeding dish. I got behind the steering wheel first. Mom grunted and climbed in the back seat. "We'll need a lookout," I said. "I'm sure the alley is roped off now."

"I can do that," Mary Ann said. "Then, if Matt finds out, I can pretend I was only walking by and saw you three up to no good." She grinned. "I'll say I tried to stop you—"

"Very funny. Matt knows you're as guilty as the rest of us."

"Maybe so, but if I talk long enough, he gets distracted with something else.

You might want to try it. Just make sure your story doesn't change."

"Are you trying to teach me how to lie?" I peered in the rearview mirror.

"No." She grinned. "Just showing you how to perfect your craft."

I never would have guessed sweet little Mary Ann was such a conniver. I shrugged. You just never could tell about a person. Look at Mrs. Worthington. Not that I knew her before, but according to Mary Ann, she had been a cowed, timid thing. Now, she radiated joy when she should be mourning.

"Park here." Mom tapped my shoulder. "We can walk over from the coffee shop. No one will suspect a thing."

No one would think twice about us parking in front of our own shop, but okay. I stopped the van and reached for the handle of the coffee shop.

"Where are you going?" Mom hissed.

"I need caffeine." I never could pass up this place, no matter what time of day it was.

"We don't have time." She dragged me across the street, around the strip of stores, and into the alley, not releasing my arm until we reached the strip of yellow crime scene tape.

"We're too late."

"For you, maybe." Mom ducked and went under, leaving the rest of us with our mouths hanging open. "What? Either I clear my name or I'm going to jail anyway. What have I got to lose?"

True. I lifted the tape and joined her. *God, forgive us for our stupidity.*

Blood splatters in the alley. Hmm. I turned in a slow circle, my gaze landing on any and everything. How much walking around should we do? If they found the blood, then they already cased the place, right? We wouldn't actually disturb a crime scene, I hoped.

Now, if I were going to bash someone in the head, where would I do it? Those little sign placards they used to photograph a crime scene weren't conveniently placed to make my job easier.

I closed my eyes and tried to imagine meeting someone in a dark alley. Someone with ill intent. Perhaps, Jim had taken out the garbage and found himself jumped. No other reason for him to be out there after dark made any sense. I opened my eyes and paced around the dumpster while Mom and Greta walked the area inside the crime scene tape. Head wounds tended to bleed a lot, so finding something shouldn't be … there!

On the cement wall next to the dumpster were the telltale rusty spots I'd come to recognize since changing my writing genre to romantic mysteries. I glanced down, noting more dotting the gravel next to a spilled box of used packing material. He had been taking out the garbage.

"Mom, did you lock the bakery the night Jim was killed?" None of us were good at setting the alarm at the house, so it wasn't unthinkable that she would have forgotten.

"Of course, I did." She glanced at the back of the building. "It would be irresponsible of me not to lock it."

"But, the lock was sticking last week," Greta said. "Did you get that fixed?"

"No." She grinned and reached for the doorknob. The door swung open. "Voila! Now, to find my rolling pin. The police may think they have it, but I've been framed. Rocking Reads isn't the only business someone wants to shut down."

With a shrug toward Mary Ann, who stood at a safe distance away with a look of alarm on her face, I joined Mom and Greta. We'd crossed one line, why not another. I ran into Greta's back and glanced over her shoulder.

Black fingerprint powder covered every surface. Boxes were out of place, supplies knocked over. Why couldn't the police be neat while searching for something? My heart ached for my mother. She took such pride in an orderly shop.

"We'll help you clean up," I said, putting an arm around her shoulder.

She sniffed. "We can't do anything until they say so. Let's find my rolling pin. I usually keep it on that top shelf for safe keeping. If the wood gets scratched, it doesn't roll right." She grabbed a step stool and set it under the shelf. She climbed up and shoved her hand into a plastic bin and gave a shout of triumph.

"This is my pin."

"Why didn't the police find it?" I took the pin while she climbed down.

Mom took a couple of steps back and, with her hands on her hips, studied the shelf. "It doesn't look like they searched anything up there. We need to find out from Officer Jones where the pin was found. If it wasn't up there, it isn't mine. They found a murder weapon and looked no further. Typical incompetence. Our town really needs a woman on the force."

"Since your back door lock is broken, anyone could have placed the weapon in here." I bit my lip. "Who knows you use that kind of rolling pin?"

She looked at me as if I were dense. "Anyone who has ever been in the shop and watched me baking."

Half the town, then. I leaned against the counter. How could I question Officer Jones without alerting him to the fact we were in the store before he gave us permission? I couldn't. My shoulders slumped. We'd have to confess.

"Let's go see Officer Jones." Feeling every bit like I was being led to the guillotine, I headed back to the alley.

Mom and Greta whispered behind me. "Is she crazy?"

"He'll lock us up."

"This is ridiculous."

Outside, Mary Ann laughed with a handsome young man in uniform. Thankfully, his back was to us. Her eyes widened, and she waved her hand to get us to hide. When he tried to turn to see what she was waving at, she grabbed his chin and forced him to look at her. *Very subtle, Mary Ann.*

We ducked behind the dumpster as she hooked her arm through his and led him away. That was close. I didn't want the first time I met the new rookie to be while breaking the law.

Once they were out of sight, I stood. "Let's go. We have to let Wayne know they have the wrong murder weapon."

"Can't you just call Matthew and let him tell them?" Mom brushed off the seat of her pants. "Officer Jones is going to scowl and arrest us for entering a crime scene. It won't matter to him that they've already checked things out. The tape is still up, and that man seems to go by the book. I have no idea why your sister has the hots for him. He's handsome, but he has the personality of a rock."

I could wait until I spoke with Matt and see what he says. He called every day or so. A few hours wouldn't hurt, right? Wayne had no idea we were at the store.

We made our way around the strip of shops and mingled on the sidewalk as if we had no sense and no place to go. My gaze kept straying to Delicious Aroma. It was never too late in the day for my favorite caffeinated beverage.

"Mrs. Nelson?" Two men in dark business suits approached us. "Owner of Heavenly Bakes?" A man with dark, slicked back hair and smelling of expensive cologne raised an eyebrow.

"That would be me." Mom wiped her hands on her thighs and extended one.

He took her hand. "Steve Larkin of Larkin Enterprises. This is my associate, Thomas Blackwell. We'd like to discuss a bit of business with you. Over coffee, perhaps?"

I recognized his voice from the bookstore. No way was Mom meeting with him alone. "We'd love, to. I'm Stormi Nelson, owner of the property. My mother owns the business."

His eyes widened. "I wasn't aware. Please, join us." He motioned his head toward Delicious Aroma.

"Well, I guess I'll find Mary Ann and hang out here on the sidewalk," Greta said, scowling. "I'm just the hired help." She stomped away.

The rest of us glanced at each other, then strolled across the street and into the coffee shop. Mr. Larkin led us to a corner table, away from the bustle and noise of the counter. "Thomas, take the ladies' drink orders, please. I need to make a phone call. I'll return in a moment. Please, excuse me."

We gave Thomas our order, then leaned close. "He didn't do his homework, if he didn't know you actually owned the real estate," Mom said. "From the look on his face, he expected me to be an easy sell. You ... not so much."

True. I straightened in my seat and studied the man talking on his cell phone across the room. He oozed money and didn't look like the type to dirty his hands by killing a man and trying to frame a middle-aged woman. I transferred my attention to Thomas. Now, the muscular sidekick looked like he could handle just about anything.

Thomas brought our coffee at the same moment Mr. Larkin joined us. "Sorry about that," Mr Larkin gave a thin-lipped smile, "but business calls.""Yes, it does." I took a sip of my frozen mocha. "What, exactly, is your business with my mother and I, Mr. Larkin?"

"Steve, please." He pulled a business card from his breast pocket and slid it across the table. "We're an investment firm that buys prime real estate and improves the quality of living in the town or city in which we purchase."

Sounded like a lot of mumbo jumbo to me. "The quality of living in Oak Meadows is excellent."

"Don't you agree that Main Street is

old-fashioned? Imagine what this town could do with a mall and more modern establishments. Why, money would flow into the commercial businesses."

"The old-fashioned feel is what draws people into settling here."

"We're offering owners more than the property is worth. We're willing to do almost anything to get what we want."

"That sounds like a threat, Steve. Let's take a look at Mrs. Worthington." I leaned my arms on the table and speared him with a glance. "How convenient that her husband died, in my mother's bakery, and she sells Rocking Reads to you immediately after. She did, right? She accepted your offer? Well, dead body or not, my mother and I are not in the market to sell."

"As for a body, I have no idea what you're talking about." His light blue eyes hardened. "If we can't get all the businesses to sell, our idea for improvement won't work."

I shrugged. "Then, Steve, you need a new idea. Thanks for the coffee." I stood and marched from the shop, leaving

Mom to follow.

"That was excellent." She clapped her hands once we reached the sidewalk. "Now, we stand back and see to what lengths that man is willing to go to get our store."

Hopefully, he wouldn't go as far as murder. "Our suspect list is growing. Mrs. Worthington is happy her husband is dead, and Steve wants our property. Both have motives for murder. The only thing that doesn't feel right is the method of getting what they want. Larkin Enterprises can't kill off every property owner here. That would be like hanging a sign around Steve's neck saying he's the killer."

Greta and Mary Ann pushed away from where they leaned against the van. "Did you learn anything?" Mary Ann asked.

"Only that we can add Steve Larkin and his henchman, Thomas, to our list of suspects." I climbed into the passenger seat. "I'm finished investigating for the day. I need to let what we've learned simmer in my mind." Maybe then, something would become clear.

Once home, I took my half-drank coffee to the backyard and stretched out on a lawnchair. Sadie laid her big head in my lap, offering comfort after a long day.

"Hey, Stormi."

I glanced up to see Tony Salazar, my neighbor, on a ladder. Being a "little" person who liked to chat over the fence, the ladder was a permanent fixture. All I could see were his hands clutching the wood and his eyes peering over. I hid a grin behind my cup. He was so cute. "Hey."

"The wife and I will take the watch tonight."

"Great."

"Especially since Mrs. Rogers is on the war path." He laughed. "She's trying to get a petition to have you run out of town. I told her you were here first and people didn't do that anymore. She said you're trying to kill her."

"She told the police the same thing." I sighed and approached the fence. "She was eavesdropping through my kitchen window and overheard me and Mary Ann talking about the plot of a book."

"Don't worry about her. Most of us like you."

"Thanks. Have fun on your walk." I patted his hand, thinking I needed to have him and his wife over for dinner sometime. Speaking of dinner, with the mood I was in, I needed to do some cooking to soothe my nerves.

"Come on, Sadie. You've been outside enough today." I let her into the kitchen where she sat and stared at every item of food I pulled from the pantry.

Dakota barreled through the back door, sliding to a halt on the asphalt before he tripped over the dog. "What's for supper?"

"Where have you been?" I glanced at the clock. Usually everyone was home by five and it was crowding six o'clock.

"Mom is working late." He put hypothetical quotes with his fingers around the word working. "Cherokee is studying with a friend," again the quotes around studying, "and I saw Grandma leave with her banker boyfriend. It's just me and you. Wanna come see what I

found?"
    "What's that?"
    "A   dropped   love   letter   by   Mrs.
Worthington to her heart throb."

7

The envelope looked as if a truck had run over it. "You opened it?"

"No." He looked taken aback. "Even I know that's against the law. I found it on the road past Main Street."

The boy did cover a lot of distance on his skateboard. I turned the envelope over in my hands. No address. Just the name Dennis Franklin in curly writing on the front. I sniffed and raised it to my nose. Was that perfume? It had to be a love letter.

I narrowed my eyes at my nephew. "How did you know I would want this?"

"Really? I can snoop with the best." He grinned and crossed his arms. "I've been listening to everything you and Grandma say. Look behind the toaster."

Why, the little sneak. Hidden behind my stainless steel toaster was a small recording device. "Why?"

"Practice. I want to be a detective like Matt. Or go into business for myself as a Private Investigator. Either way, I intend on making money solving crimes."

"Do you have any more equipment like this?"

"Spy stuff? Yeah. I have several tiny cameras that will fit almost anywhere. You can borrow whatever you like." He opened the fridge and grabbed a can of soda.

"Does your Mom buy this for you?" I couldn't see Angela spending hard cash on something she would see as frivolous.

"I've been working part-time at the electronics store. It's perfect." He saluted me with his aluminum can and headed upstairs.

While I admired his ingenuity, I really hoped he wasn't recording private moments. Such as when Mom was with Robert or Angela with whoever her latest flavor of the month was. I shuddered. Oh. He'd better not be taping me and Matt. I'd skin him alive! I glared at the ceiling as if he could hear my thoughts. Still, his equipment might come in handy someday.

I sat at the table and opened the letter.

My Dearest Dennis:
Things are progressing exactly as they should. I will have the funds in a matter of days and we can escape to a tropical place and live as if we are young lovers, frolicking in the waves. My heart yearns for the day ....

I thought I'd be sick. Being a respectable romance writer, I'd never talk like that.

When we can follow our dreams. You're such a different man than Jim. What did I ever do to get so lucky?

When the letter turned to what she wanted to do once they got together, I skipped to the signature. Ida.

I grabbed my cell phone and called Mary Ann. "What's Mrs. Worthington's first name?"

"Ida, why?"

I grinned. "I'm holding a love letter from her to one Dennis Franklin."

"The mailman? No way!"

"Yes. It's pretty disgusting, but at least we now know who the boyfriend is." I leaned back in the chair, glancing toward the stairs. I was constantly telling Dakota not to do what I was just doing. It wasn't good for the kitchen chair. "And, she mentions funds coming in soon. That has to be from the sale of the store. They plan on moving somewhere tropical."

"What are you going to do with the letter?"

"I guess I should turn it in to Wayne." After I made a copy, of course. "We want to keep him happy so he stays off our back. Who was the cutie I saw you with earlier?"

"Michael Barker. He was patrolling the street and saw me loitering in the alley." She sighed. "It took some fancy talking to divert his attention off of you guys."

The doorbell rang, sending Sadie barking like a maniac to the front of the house. She rammed the chair I was in.

My arms flailed. The chair slid out from under me. I crashed onto the floor, my cell phone skidding across the floor. I lay there and stared at the ceiling. If I didn't stop falling on my backside, I'd end up with a broken tail bone for sure.

Steps thundered down the stairs. Dakota raced into the kitchen and bent over me. "Are you all right?"

I nodded, and motioned for my phone. When he handed it to me, I gasped, "Doorbell."

"Got it."

"Stormi Nelson!" Mary Ann screeched. "If you don't answer me right now, I'm calling 911."

"My … chair … fell over." I struggled to a sitting position as Dakota shuffled into the kitchen holding a paper bag by his fingertips. "What's that?"

"Dog poop." He dropped the offending object on the table.

"Not there! Outside in the garbage." I was going to march right over and confront Mrs. Rogers once I could walk without bending over like an old woman. Who else would pull such a childish prank?

Dakota rushed to do what I'd told him. When he returned, I set him to work bleaching the table.

"I've got to go," I told Mary Ann. "See you in the morning." I hung up and glared out the front window toward Mrs. Roger's house. Her curtains were open enough for me to see her shape outlined in the window.

Dakota handed me a bag of frozen peas. "What do you want to do? I can rig some of those paper poppers in her mailbox. They might give her a heart attack."

I held the bag on my backside. "I'm not sure what to do yet, but I don't want to hurt her." Maybe I could find a Homeowners Association violation or something. But, if I retaliated, this little feud of hers could go on and on. If I were actually going to murder her, she wasn't helping her case any.

"Sorry about the lack of supper," I said, closing my curtains. "But, I'm taking a hot bath and going to bed."

"No problem. I'll call Mom and tell

her to bring me a hamburger." He bounded back up the stairs.

That boy was going to make some woman a wonderful husband someday.

As I lay in a tub of hot bubbly scented water, drinking lemonade out of a crystal wine glass, I thought of Mrs. Worthington and her sweetheart. I didn't blame her, really, especially if her husband was abusive as Mom claimed. But, would the woman kill in order to escape the abuse? It had happened before. Women reached their breaking point and killed their husbands.

I might drive Matt nuts with my snooping, but the darling man would never lay a finger on me in anger. Why couldn't people just kill each other off in books like I did?

Someone knocked on the bathroom door. I ducked under the bubbles, leaving only my face exposed. "Come in, unless you're Dakota. Then, stay out."

"It's me." Angela came in and perched on the counter. "My son showed me the love letter he found and his spy equipment." She swung her legs, staring at the floor.

I knew she had more to say. Her forehead was creased with worry wrinkles, the makeup settling into the lines and making her appear older than she was. "What's wrong?"

"Am I a bad mother?"

Wow. Not what I expected. "Why would you ask me such a thing?"

"My son has to go looking for excitement. Things that might get him killed, or worse, in trouble with the law." She kicked off her stilettos. "Your snooping has made him want to be a detective."

"There are worse things to do as a career."

"But this one is dangerous."

"Dakota is a good boy, Angela, but he's going to do what he wants to do. I wouldn't worry too much about him. I'd worry more about Cherokee. I haven't seen her in two days."

"She's working at the grocery store. I forgot to tell you." She raised her head and grinned. "My kids are both working and making good grades. I guess that does make me a good parent."

I nodded. "Anything else? The water is getting cold." Not to mention my bubbles were disappearing.

"Oh, Mom texted me wanting to know where they found her rolling pin. I did some investigating. They found it stuffed behind the toilet. Goodnight."

It sure was a good thing to have a family member who worked at the police station. Hopefully, she was discreet. As a single mother, she needed her job. I didn't charge her a lot of rent, just enough to make up for the electricity she uses with long showers and the extra food, but she still needed money of her own.

I stood and drained the water from the tub. Clues were falling into place. I might actually have Jim's death solved before Matt returned from his latest job.

I slipped on my pajamas and grabbed the latest mystery I'd purchased. Oh. I'd bought it the same day Jim was killed. I ran my hands over the red and black cover. If we'd only known.

Sliding under the covers, I said a

quick prayer for discernment and wisdom. I'd learned from prior experience that asking for God's help makes the journey a bit less rocky and the gumshoeing a bit less dangerous.

My phone rang, eliciting a smile when I recognized the number as Matt's. "I miss you."

He chuckled. "I miss you."

"How much longer?"

"No more than a week, I hope. What did you do today?"

"I'm glad you asked." I scooted against the headboard. "I need your advice. Before you get mad, hear me out."

He sighed.

"They've already processed the crime scene at the bakery, but the tape is still up. Mom and I went looking for her rolling pin—"

"I thought they found that."

"Mom was convinced it wasn't hers. She was right. Her rolling pin was right where she left it. High on a shelf in a box. The one Wayne has was found behind the toilet."

"How do you know that?"

"Uh, someone told me, or maybe I overheard it?"

He groaned. "You're killing me here. What's the advice?"

"Do I come clean with Wayne? Will he arrest us?"

"He won't arrest you. I'll tell him what you've done. I doubt he'll be too mad since they have processed the scene. I'll also ask him to take down the tape so Anne can get back to work. How's that?"

"You're the best boyfriend ever."

"I know."

I told him about the love letter with promises to turn it in to Wayne in the morning. He congratulated me on what I'd discovered so far, but pressed on me the seriousness of being careful.

"This person has killed once already," he said, "for something as trivial as a storefront. If they find out how close you're getting to knowing their identity, you could be in real danger. I'll ask Wayne to keep a better eye on you. He's going to be my new partner when I return, anyway."

"Does he know that?"

"Yes."

"That must have given him the chills. Your last partner got killed because of me."

"He was a dirty cop." Sorrow laced his words. "A good man who sold out. It wasn't your fault."

"He acted the way he did, because his family needed something. Don't be too harsh on Koontz. I'd be dead if not for him."

"And for that, I'll be forever grateful to him. Goodnight, sweetheart. I love you."

"I love you, too."

We hung up, leaving me to wonder how his partnership with Wayne was going to affect my snooping and my sister's crush. I figured it would be torture for me, and Angela would be on cloud nine, drooling every time the man came over. And he would come over on a regular basis. When Matt was in town, he spent a lot of time at my house.

I grinned. I might be able to have some fun with the big guy, knowing that

whatever I did would, in some small way,
make his life a little more exasperating.

8

The next morning, I locked the front door and set the alarm since everyone else had already gone their separate ways. Mom got the okay to return to the bakery, Angela went to the station, and the kids to school. I was on my way to pick up Mary Ann for our first visit of the day. As I headed for my car, I glanced toward Mrs. Rogers house.

She stood out front in a faded housedress and watered a myriad of flowers. I took a deep breath for courage and headed her way.

When she saw me approaching, she aimed the water hose in my direction like a weapon. "Don't come any closer. I'm not afraid to use this."

I shook my head. "I'm not afraid to get wet." The last thing I wanted was to start my day soaking, but I wouldn't give her the satisfaction of knowing that. I held out my hands. "I just want to talk. I'm unarmed."

She raised the hose a little higher. "So, talk. I'm keeping this aimed right where it is."

"I've been informed that you've been eavesdropping and heard something you shouldn't." I kept my gaze glued to the hose in her hand.

"I think I heard exactly what I needed to hear." Her hose-holding hand twitched. "Now, I can be on my guard against a murdering romance author such as yourself."

"Mrs. Rogers, please." I tilted my head and implored with my eyes for her to understand. "You've been, shall we say, opinionated and difficult?" I held up a hand to halt her protests. "We both know you have, so don't deny it. What you heard was merely the plot of another mystery novel with the victim modeled after you." I grinned. "It was a harmless way for me to let slide your over-the-top grievances against me. I promise not to use your real name in my book."

"Don't patronize me! I know that you write your books after real life crimes, and I don't intend to be your next bestseller." She raised the hose. "Get off my property."

The hose hit me full in the face with the force of a sledgehammer. Water went up my nose and in my mouth. I slipped to the grass. She continued to spray as I struggled to my feet, my shoes sliding on the grass like a cartoon character trying to run and getting nowhere.

"Get out!"

I fled her screeching as if bullets followed until I leaned against my Mercedes to catch my breath. The woman was insane. I glanced across the street. "I'm filing a police report!" I wrung out my hair and stomped back into the house to change.

When I exited again, fifteen minutes later, with dry clothes and wet hair, Mary Ann was coming up the sidewalk. I glared at where Mrs. Rogers had stood across the street and slid into my car where I waited for Mary Ann to join me.

Where had the old bat gone?

"I thought you were picking me up?" she said.

"I was, but the witch across the street sprayed me with the hose." I turned the key in the ignition. "Like I was a stray dog taking a doodie on her lawn." I roared from the driveway and down the street, hoping, praying, there were no police officers around.

"Where are we going first?"

I tightened my grip on the steering wheel and slowed down. "The police station. I'm filing a complaint and turning over the letter."

"Did you talk to Matt?"

"Yes. He advised I turn it over." I cut her a sideways glance. "Did you know that Wayne is now his partner?"

She gave a sheepish grin. "Yeah, but I didn't know how to tell you. It's more fun to watch the two of you bicker."

Good grief. I parked in front of the station and marched to the front door.

Angela glanced up from her desk. "Officer Jones is busy."

"How did you know I was here to see

him?” I glanced toward his office.

“Because Mrs. Rogers is here.”

This was so unfair. “We’ll wait.” I sat on a hard plastic chair and crossed my arms. I should file a charge against her for assault. But, I had stepped off the sidewalk onto her lawn. Would that void any complaint I had?

The door to Wayne’s office opened. Mrs. Rogers sauntered out looking like the proverbial cat who swallowed the canary. At least she had changed her housedress for polyester pants and a floral blouse. She gave me a smug look and waltzed out the door.

I bolted from my seat and down the hall to Wayne’s office. “I want to file a complaint.”

“Join the club.” He waved me toward a seat. “Please stay off Mrs. Rogers’s lawn.”

“She assaulted me. All I wanted to do was make amends.”

He steepled his fingers. “Look, Stormi. She’s a lonely old woman with nothing to do and no friends. Harassing you gives her purpose. Let it go.”

Well, when he put it that way. "Fine. I'll try. But that isn't the only reason I'm here." I dug the letter out of my pocket and slid it across his desk. "My nephew found this while skateboarding, and since he knows I'm working this case, brought me the letter."

"You are not working the case." He narrowed his eyes. "You're snooping."

I shrugged. "Whatever."

"Thank you for bringing this in. Matt told me you had it." He stared across the desk. "Did you make a copy?"

Duh. I raised my eyebrows. I knew what he was silently screaming at me and it had nothing to do with the letter. "We went into the bakery and found mom's rolling pin. The one you have is not hers. Are you going to arrest us?"

"I should, but I won't." He straightened. "That, and the letter, are actually very good evidence. Have you ever thought of becoming a police officer?"

"Wow, is that a compliment?"

"You can go now."

I stood, grinning. "Yes, sir. I shall

return with more evidence."

His loud sigh followed me from the room. My mood was definitely lighter when I joined Mary Ann in the lobby. Wayne Jones actually thought I'd make a good police officer. While nice to know, I preferred putting words to paper and snooping without the strigent rules police had to follow.

"What did he say?" Mary Ann asked as we headed back to my car.

"To leave Mrs. Rogers alone because she doesn't have a life, and that I should consider becoming a police officer. I'm that good." I grinned and got into the car.

"He said that?"

"Yep." She didn't have to sound so surprised. I could be good at more than crafting a story, couldn't I? "Are you ready to head back toward Mrs. Worthington's?"

"As ready as ever."

We stopped for our morning java and headed to where I believed the reason for Jim's death lived. Instead of parking in her driveway, I stopped on the side of the country highway. Before confronting the happy widow again, I wanted to visit a couple of her neighbors and find out a bit more on the married life of being a Worthington.

I stared through the window at the houses on either side of Mrs. Worthington's. While still cute and in good repair, neither could match Ida's for being adorable. "Do you have any idea who lives in the other houses?"

Mary Ann dug in her purse and pulled out a small notebook. "I've been doing some research. In the green house lives a Mrs. Davidson, widowed, lives with adult son, and actively involved in her church. Rumor is that he sells pot on the side, but nothing has ever been done about it. The other house, is an elderly couple. Retired truck drivers, Alma and Fred Denney."

"I knew it was a good idea to hire you." Most of the time, she knew what I needed before I did.

"Look." She grabbed my arm. "It seems as if Ida is getting a personal delivery."

My stomach turned at the public

display of affection. Mr. Franklin had Ida pressed so close that from a distance they almost looked like one person. I never would have thought the portly mailman could be such a Casanova. "I'm a little disgusted."

"Unless we want to be seen, we're stuck in the car until they either go in the house or Mr. Franklin leaves."

I was not good at the stake-out part of solving crimes. Too boring. I leaned my head back against the seat and wished I'd thought to bring my camera. Who knew if photos of those two in a heated embrace would mean anything to the police? Wait. I had one on my cell phone.

Just as I remembered I had a camera on my phone, Mr. Franklin climbed into his mail vehicle and drove away. Ida watched him until he was out of sight before entering her house.

Having used a regular camera for so long, I tended to forget the one on my cell phone was actually of better quality. I sighed and grabbed my purse. Mary Ann and I headed for the greenhouse.

I raised my hand to rap on the door,

only to have it yanked open before I connected. "Hello? Mrs. Davidson?"

An overweight woman in sweats glared from under a mop of unruly gray curls. "If you're here to see Phil, he ain't here."

A strong pet odor escaped the house, slamming me in the face. I took a step back. "No, ma'am, we're here to ask you a few questions. I'm Stormi Nelson, and this is Mary Ann Steele. We're investigating the death of Jim Worthington, and—"

"The police were already here asking questions. I had nothing to tell them then, and I've nothing to tell them now."

"We aren't with the police. I'm a romantic mystery writer of true crime. May we come in?"

She stepped out and closed the door. "No, you may not. I haven't cleaned up for visitors. Have a seat on the porch." She moved a box of gardening tools and a stack of old newspapers, revealing a couple of weathered wicker furniture. "If you're here to help Ida, I doubt she wants your help."

"Why do you say that?"

She lowered her bulk into a chair and leaned close, the smell of mildew and onions wafting from her clothes. "Because that woman is happier than a pig in … well, you know. There's no need for me to be vulgar."

Thank God for that. "We've heard rumors that Mr. Worthington was abusive to Ida. Is that true?"

"That's a fact." She sighed. "That girl couldn't come out of her house for days sometimes because of the bruises. But then again, why'd she need to? That mailman has been making a stop at her house around lunchtime every day for months. Jim might have slapped her around a bit, but she was getting her love from another man. Ain't proper." She leaned closer. "I've seen other men come and go. That woman is a regular floozy. You ought to write a book about her. She dressed all plain when her husband was home, but once he left, the fancy clothes came out. I think those men were giving her gifts. Ain't fornicating against the law?"

I met Mary Ann's surprised gaze. So, the battered wife was seeing other men. If I'd been Jim, I might have wanted to hit her too. "Did Jim know?"

"He'd have been blind not to," Mrs. Davidson said. "But he spent so much time at that store of his, he wasn't taking care of his wife's needs. It was a regular occurrence to hear yelling come from that house. No love lost on either part is my guess. Now, me and my husband, we loved each other. He didn't even care that I wasn't the best housekeeper or that I had put on a few pounds. I always felt sorry for the Worthingtons." She pointed a pudgy finger at my face. "If you find a good man, you love him, love him good, understand?"

I leaned back. "Yes, ma'am." I fully intended to.

"That's good." She stared across the street. "So, you're a writer."

"Yes."

She nodded. "Got any erotica in them books? Because I could give you some pointers from my married life."

"No, not at all." I needed to change

the subject, and fast. "Do you think Ida hated Jim enough to kill him?"

9

"Of course she did," Mrs. Davidson said. "She's about to come into a lot of money with the sell of that store." She heaved her bulk out of her chair. "My soaps are coming on. I don't miss them for anything. Good luck with your research." With those words, she disappeared into the house.

Still, the woman had been a wealth of information. I couldn't wait to talk with the other neighbors.

We moved quickly down the side of the road and approached the Denney house. Mrs. Denney, gray-haired, at least five foot ten and smiling, greeted us before we reached the house. "Bless my stars, it's Stormi Nelson."

I grinned at Mary Ann. A fan!

"Come in, come in." She held a red-painted door wide open. "Sit, sit." She motioned toward a floral sofa in a spotless living room. "Fred! It's Stormi Nelson. We read all of your books."

"Thank you." A warm flush washed over me. I'd never get over the thrill of meeting a new fan.

"Fred!" she barked. "I have no idea what is keeping that man." She perched her thick frame on the edge of an easychair.

While not fat, Alma Denney had muscles to rival any man's. She had to be crowding sixty, but oozed energy and strength. In her sleeveless tee shirt and jeans, she did not look like the type of woman who liked flowers and doilies, yet her house was full of such things and a floral incense filled the room. I liked her immediately.

"We're investigating Jim Worthington's death, and would like to ask you a few questions."

"Sure, sure." She jumped up. "Let me get you some tea and sandwiches."

She rushed from the room, returning minutes later with a porcelain tea pot and small cucumber sandwiches. "My grandma, being an immigrant from England, told me to always be prepared for company. If Fred and I aren't on the road, I've got delicacies such as these for occasions such as this. Glad to share. Fred!"

I bit back a giggle at the way she continued to yell out her husband's name and reached for a sandwich. "Did you witness physical abuse between Ida and Jim?"

"Sure, sure, everyone did. I started to call the cops once, but Fred told me to mind my own business. The man was only trying to put his cheating wife into place, my Fred said." She shrugged. "Still doesn't warrant a man hitting a woman. No, it doesn't."

"Was there anything else strange about their marriage? Do you think Ida could commit murder?"

"No way." She shoved two finger sandwiches into her mouth. "I saw that woman release a spider from her house to the yard. Her morals might be messed up, but she isn't brave. The only beef I got with her is that she doesn't seem to care about our good Lord. No, no, I've tried talking to her several times and she wants nothing to do with salvation. So, I pray for her. Fred!"

Mary Ann giggled. "He walked past the kitchen door. I guess he isn't interested in visiting with a couple of women."

"Sure he is." She jumped up again and slammed the door open. "Fred, where are you going? Let Dennis Franklin mow Ida's lawn. Bless your heart, you big galoot." She turned back to us, grinning. "He just can't let a poor widow do her own lawn work. That's the kind of man he is. He goes over there almost every day to help with one thing or another."

My heart sank. What if Fred was one of Ida's visitors? Poor Alma, or poor Fred, if you think about it. The woman would crush him like a soda can. "Well, I thank you for your time, but we've really got to be going."

"You must come back when Fred has time to meet you."

"We will. Thank you." While we

didn't learn a lot of new information, we did learn enough to warrant another visit with Ida.

"What's up?" Mary Ann asked once we were hiking at a fast pace toward Ida's house.

"I have a sneaking suspicion that our poor widow entertained several men while her husband was gone, and that dear Fred is one of them."

"No." Mary Ann gasped.

I nodded. "See?"

I pointed to where Fred glanced around before entering a side door on Ida's house. I'd heard of housewives turning tricks for extra money, but thought that only happened in books or on television. The petite blond widow was nothing more than a lady of the evening, err afternoon. What little compassion I might have felt for her flew out the window.

At least in my last mystery the prostitutes didn't pretend to be anything but what they were. This one made me feel as if I needed a shower. I sent a prayer for protection against immorality heavenward and approached Ida's house.

I told Mary Ann to ring the doorbell while I hid around back. I intended to catch Fred and give him a piece of my mind. Sure enough, several seconds after Mary Ann pressed the bell, Fred barged out the side door.

I stepped in front of him, crossed my arms, and glared. "Fred Denney! You should be ashamed of yourself. Seriously? You have a woman right over there who loves you and is proud of you. This will wound her."

"Alma scares the dickens out of me." He frowned. "You've seen her. You must understand."

"That's the biggest reason why you should behave. If she finds out you're tom-catting over here, she'll rip off your head." I pointed toward his house. "Now get home. If I find out you've come over here, no matter how innocent, I'll tell your wife what you're really up to."

He nodded and ran.

I joined Mary Ann and Ida on the front porch. No pleasantries, no smiles. I really didn't know what to say.

"Oh, stop glaring." Ida huffed. "So, you know my secret. It's just a part-time job and keeps me in nice clothes and jewelry. I sure couldn't rely on Jim to buy me those things, the cheapskate."

"It's against the law, Mrs. Worthington." Mary Ann looked shocked.

"Just because you're a police officer's sister, don't pretend you're all peaches and cream. This little town might look sweet and picturesque, but it's full of deceit and greed. Why shouldn't I get my share? People are bad. It's time the two of you figured that out."

"I refuse to believe that." I leaned against the aluminum siding. "I choose to believe that the majority of people are good." Otherwise, why bother trying to live as my faith prompted? "We all sin, we all make mistakes, but others, like you, step over that line. Did you kill your husband?"

"No, and I don't know who did." She sighed. "No matter what you think of me and my choice of livestyle, I'm a kind person incapable of murder. Good day."

She turned and stormed into the house.

"I guess you have more evidence to tell Officer Jones." Mary Ann headed for the car.

I followed, not exactly sure what to do about the information regarding Ida. If I turned her in, how many marriages would be ruined? Wouldn't it be better to let things ride and wait until she left town with Dennis Franklin? I really needed to snuggle on the couch with Matt and discuss this case.

We stopped by Heavenly Bakes before heading home. I hoped one of Mom's moist cupcakes would soothe my troubled spirit.

"What's up?" she asked the moment I perched on a stool. She always could tell when something was tugging at me.

I told her all that had transpired that day and how it had affected my mood, pulling me low. "I know I shouldn't let what others do affect me so much, but this morning took me by surprise."

Mom patted my arm. "That's because you have a sweet spirit. Even though you write about this stuff and snoop into people's secrets to find killers, you still believe in the good in the world. That's who you are. Don't change."

"Thanks, Mom." Tears pricked my eyes. "How's business?"

"Booming." She grinned. "Once people found out a dead body had been found in the store, they fight to get in the door. I don't let anyone see the vat unless they buy a cupcake or a cookie."

I sighed.

"Don't act like that. I'm just taking advantage of something out of my control." Mom turned on her commercial mixer and spoke over the noise. "People talk when they come in here."

I perked up. "Yeah?"

"Mostly nonsense, but the one thing that sticks out is that every business on this street is being bugged by those investors to sell."

"They're doing everything to convince the owners to sell except physically twist their arms," Greta said. "I've run them out of here twice already, once at the barrel of my pistol. But they're like a sore thumb, they keep getting in the way."

Maybe Mary Ann and I needed to pay a visit to the other Main Street businesses. The more I questioned Ida, the less I thought she killed her husband. If Steve Larkin is being a pest, maybe I should switch my attention to him.

I licked the butter cream frosting from my chocolate cupcake and let my mind wander. Suspect number one, Ida Worthington, who wanted freedom from her husband. Of course, his killer could be one of her customers, but why? What would one of them gain from her husband's death? It wasn't as if his being alive had stopped their visits.

Suspect number two, Steve Larkin. He stood to gain a lot of money if the stores on Main Street sold their property.

Then what? Would he modernize the street and lease back to the prior owners so they could resume their business or lease to a list of entirely new businesses more suited to whatever purpose he wanted to modernize for?

"This case is so twisted." I shoved the last bite of chocolate richness into my mouth.

"Are you writing everything down?" Mom asked.

"Yes. Every night before I go to bed, I make sure my notes are up to date. Every time I'm convinced I know who the killer is, something happens to make me unsure." I hopped off the stool. "At least once I do figure it out, I'll most likely be right beyond a doubt."

"That's one way of looking at it." She grinned.

"What's another?"

"That you're looking in the wrong direction."

"You think so?"

"No. My gut tells me it has something to do with the selling of these businesses. We'll keep asking around, and you keep pounding the pavement."

My thoughts exactly. No matter how frustrating the search might be, I always caught my man—or woman. I just hoped this time it wasn't when they tried to kill me.

10

"I'm heading across the street for another coffee." I hopped off the stool. "Anyone want anything?" They all shook their heads no.

Mary Ann pulled out her cell phone and started playing a game where she matched balls of the same color. "I'll take my break."

Ha ha. Like I worked her so hard she needed breaks.

I stepped outside and raised my face to the sun, letting the rays clean me of the ugliness of Ida's lifestyle. I wouldn't judge her, but I would do my best not to have to go visit her again.

"Miss Nelson?"

I opened my eyes to see Steve Larkin and his goon Thomas approaching. Just what I needed. I forced a smile. "How may I help you?"

"Have you thought any more about my offer?"

"You haven't made an offer, Mr. Larkin. You made a proposition. All we exchanged was air time and words." I glanced longingly toward the coffee shop.

"I'm willing to offer you half a million dollars for your property."

I whipped my head back in his direction hard enough to give me whiplash. Perhaps it was time to visit Jane Weston and see what the property was actually worth. Not that I would sell, and I prayed none of the other owners would either, but the amount was tempting. A petition might help. If every store owner signed, we could get Steve Larkin off our backs.

"We aren't selling." I squared my shoulders and met his hard gaze straight on.

"Be reasonable, Miss Nelson. I already own the store next to you. It's only a matter of time before I own the others. Crime is escalating in this town.

People are going to want a mall;. a place with security guards. Small town streets and quaint little shops are a thing of the past."

"Not around here." I took a step closer to him. "Please do not approach me with an offer again. I have your number. If I should suddenly come down with a case of insanity, I'll call you."

"You don't know who you're dealing with."

"I think I do." My smile widened. "Good day, gentlemen."

With long strides and my head held high, I crossed the street and entered Delicious Aroma. The first person I saw was my friend, Norma. Former prostitute and now chairman of an organization to help get women off the streets, we had hit it off almost immediately. I made a beeline for the table she sat at and motioned to her son, Tyler, the barrista, that I would have my usual.

"It seems like ages," I said, sitting down. "What have you been up to?"

She crossed one shapely leg over the other. "I purchased this place," she waved a manicured hand, "last week."

"That's wonderful! I didn't know you were interested in becoming a business owner."

She shrugged. "I didn't know I was either, but when Tyler came home and said the owners wanted to retire, they offered it to me first. Now, those vultures you were talking to outside want to offer me an astronomical amount to buy it. I haven't even had time to enjoy being a business owner."

"Are you going to sell?"

"No way." She winked. "I kind of like the idea of being a respectable business owner."

"Would you sign a petition to run the investors out of Oak Meadows?"

"In a heartbeat."

Tyler brought my drink and I fished ten dollars out of my pocket. "Keep the change. You'll need it now that your mother owns the place."

"Very cute," Norma said. "Maybe you should write comedy. So, what's the latest on you?"

I explained to her my investigating

and writing about Jim's death and what his wife did in her spare time. "I have to admit to my naivety. I had no idea that kind of stuff went on in suburbia."

"It happens a lot," she said. "Makes it hard for those on the streets to make a living, that's for sure." She tapped her nails on the table top. "At least you aren't dressed in disguise trying to get yourself killed this time. That hunky boyfriend of yours must be happy."

"He's been out of town on assignment." I sipped my drink. "I miss him."

"Who wouldn't?" She laughed. "If Matthew Steele would have been the first man God created, God would have said, 'I've attained perfection' and the rest of us would never have been thought of. Matt is so perfect, he would never have eaten that fruit, and I'm not just talking about the way he looks."

"Don't let him hear you say that. Matt's ego is big enough." I was a lucky woman. I stood. "I need to get home. I try to do some writing in the afternoons and my snooping in the mornings."

"Good luck. Hit me up when you've got that petition going."

I stepped outside, fully intending to return to the bakery to fetch Mary Ann, when I saw Thomas duck into the alley. Since the man rarely left his boss's side, his actions made my snoop radar twang.

I jogged across the street and into the alley between the bookstore and the drugstore. This wasn't the dark, dingy alley of espionage movies. The alleys behind the stores on Main Street was empty of all but cars belonging to the owners, dumpsters, and the occasional stray cat. Along one edge was a cement wall. The sun lit up the area as bright as Main Street and yet I still managed to lose sight of Thomas.

After glancing both ways, I decided to turn to my right. If I didn't find him before I reached the back of Heavenly Bakes, I'd enter the backdoor and get Mary Ann to come home with me so we could get to work.

Halfway down on the wall, sprayed with red paint were the words, "Sell and get out". Usually, I would think the message was directed at me, but this time, I knew it targeted every one of the businesses lining that alley. I touched the paint. Still wet. As I started to turn, something hit me in the back of the head. I fell, my head bouncing off the asphalt. Everything went dark.

"Stormi."

I opened my eyes and stared into Matt's worried face. "I must be dead."

He smiled. "You're very much alive." He put his arms around me and helped me sit up against the nearest car. "What happened?"

"You're here." I touched the back of my head, my fingers coming away red. I was bleeding! No, wait, it was red paint.

"That isn't why you're lying on the ground."

"Someone hit me. I was following Thomas and I stopped to see the painted letters on the wall. When I turned to leave, someone clobbered me."

"An ambulance is on the way," Mom said, squatting beside us. "When you didn't return after getting your coffee, and Mary Ann couldn't find you, she called Matthew. Who is Thomas?"

I narrowed my eyes. "You were home?"

"I wanted to surprise you."

"You did." I tried to stand. "Now, take me home, and I'll explain everything. I don't need the ambulance."

Matt helped me to my feet. "You probably have a concussion."

"Won't be the first and probably not the last." My stomach rolled. I bent over and lost my breakfast as the ambulance came to a stop at the head of the alley. Before I could protest further, I was on a gurney and rolled away.

"Wait." I held out my hand. "Matt."

"I'm coming, sweetheart." He turned and said something to Mom and his sister, then jogged to catch up. He swung into the back of the ambulance and rode with us to the hospital.

Since the movement of the gurney and riding in the back of the ambulance increased my nausea, I kept my eyes closed until the paramedics wheeled me to a curtained alcove in the hospital and left.

"I'm glad you're here." I held my hand out to Matt.

He entwined his fingers with mine. "Me, too. Everything wrapped up just fine on the case." He sighed. "Do I need to restate the importance of not going anywhere alone when you're researching?"

"No. I think I'll remember now." But, to my credit, I hadn't expected to get whacked in broad daylight.

A nurse entered and took my vitals, a doctor came in and looked at the bump on my head and shined a light in my eyes, then wrote me a prescription for pain medication. "You've got a concussion. You'll have a headache for a day or two, but no major damage was done. Try to rest for a few days."

"See?" I glanced at Matt. "He didn't tell us anything we didn't already know. Now, how are we going to get home?"

"I'm your chauffeur." Wayne Jones popped his head into the cubicle.

I groaned. "Maybe I should stay here for a few days." Once I found out he was Matt's new partner, I knew I'd see more of the man, but spending time with him while enduring a raging headache was not going to be easy.

Wayne pulled aside the privacy curtain and pushed in a wheelchair. "Ready? There are benefits to being brought in by two police officers. Speedy paperwork."

Matt helped me into the chair and wheeled me out to the parking lot where a squad car waited. "I am not riding in the back of that unless I'm wearing handcuffs."

"You aren't going to." Wayne laughed and opened the door to a Dodge Charger. "I'm off duty, although I am surprised you haven't had to ride in one before."

"Very funny." I climbed into the backseat of his car and laid down.

Matt slid in beside me, had me turn around and rested my head in his lap. "Let me take care of you."

Oh, be still my heart. "Gladly."

He smoothed the hair away from my face and caressed the area between my eyes, as Wayne drove us to my house.

When we stopped, Matt scooped me into his arms, told Wayne the code to the alarm, which it turned out hadn't been set, and carried me inside once the door was open. After depositing me on the sofa, he headed to the kitchen, returning moments later with a tall glass of diet coke.

He handed me the drink and the prescription to Wayne. "Would you get this filled, please?"

Maybe I should get injured more often. Matt was as caring as he could be and it got rid of Wayne for at least twenty minutes. I pulled a crocheted afghan over me and snuggled in for the duration.

"I missed you," I told Matt. "I worried every single second."

He knelt beside me. "No more so than I." He slid an arm under my neck and pulled me close for a kiss.

I closed my eyes, reveling in the sweetness, the softness of his kiss. Wait. I jerked upright. "Where's Sadie?" My dog always greeted me when I came home.

Matt's face hardened. "Stay here."

Grabbing a throw pillow to clutch,

and possibly use as a weapon, I waited for Matt to return and prayed my sweet Sadie was all right. If I had had an intruder, the big galoot was most likely hiding under the bed.

Footsteps thumped overhead, hopefully Matt's. I sat up straighter at the sound of nails scratching against the wood floor. Sadie barreled into the living room and washed my face with her tongue.

"She was locked in your room." A muscle ticked in Matt's jaw. "Your office is trashed and your laptop gone."

"It's a good thing I keep my notebook of clues in the kitchen." I was getting used to criminals searching my office to discover what I knew. My heart ached at my laptop being stolen, but I uploaded everything to a jumpdrive before turning it off each night. My stories were safe.

"What is it going to take to get you and your family to set the alarm?"

"I was distracted this morning." I told him how Mrs. Rogers assaulted me with the water hose. "We've been doing better, honestly."

He shook his head and pulled his cell phone from his pocket. "It's a good thing I love you, Stormi Nelson. Because otherwise, you'd drive me insane."

I grinned. "Yeah. A good thing."

Smile fading, I glanced at the ceiling. During the last crime I'd insisted on investigating, my family and I had gone to the mountains to escape a violent gang. Were we in danger of having to go into hiding again?

11

I didn't remember closing my eyes, but when I opened them, the sun was streaming through the living room window. I tossed the afghan off me and slowly swung my legs to the floor. So far, so good.

Without too much trembling, I managed to make my way to the kitchen. Mom stirred a pan on the stove.

"Good morning. I'm making you some oatmeal." She waved the wooden spoon toward one of the kitchen chairs. "Sit. Matthew slept in the easy chair last night, but I sent him home this morning. How are you feeling?"

"Like someone hit me in the head." I propped an elbow on the table and rested my head in my hands. There was so much I wanted to do today, mainly going store-to-store getting signatures. While I could maybe manage, it wouldn't be smart to go alone in case I got woozy. I could take Mary Ann, but taking another business owner might be wiser. The shop owners could relate better to someone in their same predicament.

"Mom, will you help me take a petition down Main Street today?"

"Why not wait a day or two and rest?" She plopped oatmeal into a bowl and drizzled honey over the top before handing it to me.

"Something tells me that every day counts. I feel an urgency to stop Larkin's attempts at destroying our town and in finding Jim's killer." I couldn't fully explain why the feeling, just that something big was going to happen and I needed to do something before it did.

"Okay." She sat across from me. "But once you start feeling sick, we're coming home."

"I promise to sit a lot."

"Maybe we should use Greta's old wheelchair again."

"No." I wasn't in disguise as an old

woman handing out religious tracks to prostitutes anymore as a ruse to uncover clues. I'd go to the businesses as myself. I'd even wear something nice.

"We'll go right after breakfast." She jumped up and set the pan in the sink. Filling it with water, she turned back to me. "Take your gun."

"I don't think it's come to that." I did keep my Tazer in my purse, but the little pink Glock could stay in the safe.

"Someone clobbered you, or have you forgotten?" She turned off the water.

"We'll be safe going from store-to-store. Dress professional." After a few bites of the oatmeal, I pushed the bowl away and headed to my room to get dressed.

Being a full-time author, I spent most of my days in some form of jeans and tee shirts, but I did have some nicer things for occasions such as meeting with my agent or attending conferences. I flipped through the clothing hanging in my closet and chose a pair of black slacks and a crisp white blouse. Pull my hair back, clip on some nice jewelry, and I was ready to go, not to mention exhausted.

I slumped on the edge of my bed. Mom would take one look at my face and refuse to drive me anywhere. I exhaled sharply and pushed to my feet. It was going to take strength and willpower to get through the day.

"Ready?" Mom, wearing a red dress with white polka-dots, looked as if she'd stepped out of the pages of a 1950s fashion magazine. Beautiful, but out of our time period.

I shrugged. "Yep." I grabbed my purse from the foyer table, along with the clipboard, and forced my legs to remain steady as I made my way to Mom's minivan. Once inside, I breathed deep and reached for the seatbelt.

"You're not feeling well." Mom glared.

"I'm fine. Let's go."

"If you collapse, I'm telling Matthew." She climbed behind the wheel and drove to the alley behind Heavenly Bakes where she continued her lecture as to how I should wait a day or two before doing anymore investigations. "I am perfectly capable of taking the petition around."

"I want to ask questions."

"I can do that, too."

"Mom, please." I shoved the door open and slid to the ground. I counted to three, giving my legs time to steady themselves, then headed for the bakery's back door. We could cut across the street and get Norma's signature first, allowing me the opportunity for coffee.

"Good morning." Greta looked up from where she mixed batter in the very vat they had found Jim's body in.

My stomach protested. "Please tell me you had that professionally cleaned."

"Of course, we did." She scowled. "Twice. I wanted to purchase a new one, but Anne said we couldn't afford it. It would have been money well spent in my opinion."

Mine, too. "I'm stealing Mom for a few hours. Can you handle things here?"

"Sure. Why is she dressed like Donna Reed from Father Knows Best?"

"I thought I looked nice." Mom smoothed her dress.

"You do, for someone from another century. I'm pretty sure my mother had a dress just like that."

Mom waved off her comment, handed me a pain pill and a water bottle from her cavernous purse, and then headed for the front door. "Let's do this so Stormi can get to bed."

As if she could read my thoughts, Mom headed straight for Delicious Aroma and made a beeline past the line to the counter. "We need to see Norma immediately."

Tyler pointed to a table in the corner and continued serving the next customer. Without glancing up, he told me he'd have my order ready as soon as he could.

"Sign this, please." Mom grabbed the clipboard from my hands and thrust it at Norma.

Norma raised her eyebrows and glanced at me.

"She thinks I'm dying and need to get straight home to bed." I made a circular motion to the side of my head behind Mom's back. Childish, but it made Norma giggle.

"You might want to try a different approach at the other shops," she said. "Maybe explain a bit more what this is about."

"We plan on it." I sat down to wait on my drink and gain a bit of strength. "I want to ask questions that Mom's speedy delivery won't allow." I patted the seat next to me. "Come on. We aren't in a hurry."

She sighed and sat next to me. "I just worry about you."

"I know."

"What kind of questions are you going to ask?" Norma said. "I told you all I knew yesterday."

"I want to know if anything strange has happened around your shop. Yesterday, someone painted a warning on the wall behind the stores across the street, then hit me in the head. I have a concussion. That's what Mom is all worked up over."

Norma took her top lip between her teeth and stared toward the counter. "Yesterday, I had to pick Tyler up from work because two of his tires were flat.

Not slashed, just flat. I thought at first maybe it was because they're old, but now … I'm not so sure. Why would two tires go flat at once? One back and one front?"

I motioned for Mom to write that down. She flipped to a page toward the bottom of the stack on the clipboard and started writing.

"Have you heard about anything else weird happening?" I smiled at Tyler as he brought me my frozen mocha. He declined money, saying his mom declared my drinks were on the house. "Thank you," I told her.

"No problem." She shook her head. "People still don't talk to me much. It's going to take them a while to get over my past."

"Their loss." I stood and gave her a hug before taking my drink outside with me.

"Let's get Robert's signature," Mom said. "It's his break."

I was pretty sure Mom's banker boyfriend would see her any time she waltzed into the bank, but since I didn't have a schedule other than visiting all ten of the shops lining this section of Main Street, I waved her forward. We could visit the other shops that branched off of Main onto First another day. We'd be visiting eighteen in all, not counting the bank and Rocking Reads.

The red-bricked bank was halfway down the street on our left. With vintage pony lights and the original woodwork, it was a thing of beauty. What would happen to it if Steve Larkin had his way? Or the library at the end of First Street? Both were historical buildings that helped define our town and remind us of the grandeur of days past. I couldn't let them be destroyed.

Mom led me through the bank lobby and straight to Robert Smithfield's office. The slight-build, balding man beamed at the sight of her. I needed to find time to get to know him better. If he was going to become a permanent fixture in my mother's life, I needed to make sure he didn't plan on breaking her heart.

Robert greeted Mom with a kiss and me with a shake of the hand. "What brings the two loveliest ladies in Oak Meadows to my office?"

"We want you to sign this." Mom handed him the clipboard.

"Certainly." He scanned the words on the page and signed his signature with a flourish. "You could be asking for my house and I'd give it to you, my dear, but this is also something I gladly sign."

"Has Larkin Enterprises been bothering the bank?" I lowered myself into a stuffed leather chair.

"Not us, but the shops around us." Robert pulled out a chair for Mom, then moved to his seat behind his polished mahogany desk. "If the shops go, so will the bank. Our largest investors are the shops." He folded his arms on the desktop. "I'm hearing things, Stormi. Things that bother me, and I'm not talking about your knock on the head or Jim Worthington's death. No, these, if they'd happened at any other time, might be tossed aside as childish pranks."

"Go on." I took the clipboard from Mom.

"You're getting it second hand from

me," he said. "But, make it a priority to talk to Seth Bridger at the drugstore and Nancy Caldwell at the boutique, for starters." He reached across the desk and took Mom's hand. "You be careful, Anne. You, too, Stormi. Things are heating up around town. There's a storm coming and I don't want you caught in it."

He might have been speaking to Mom, but his gaze caught mine. Whatever Robert knew, he didn't want to say in front of my mother. I nodded. "Mom, I really need a glass of water. Would you mind?"

"Oh." She pulled her hand free of Robert's. "Sure. I'll be right back."

The moment she was gone, Robert slumped back in his chair. "Larkin Enterprises has recently deposited a large sum of money in Ida Worthington's bank account. Not only that, but they've made a rather large deposit of their own." He speared me with his gaze. "There's enough money in that account to buy out this town twice over. You're playing with the big boys, Stormi."

Ants seemed to climb up and down my arms and it had nothing to do with the pain medication. "What do you suggest?"

"I don't know. But, you can't let them take over. You need to convince the town to stand firm. They're offering business owners half of what their property is worth. The amount is still significant enough to have people thinking twice about it."

"I've been offered five hundred thousand."

He shook his head. "Your shop location is worth over a million dollars. Someone has already died over this. Please, don't let the next be you or Anne."

I swallowed past the mountain in my throat. This time, I might be tackling a monster I couldn't win against.

12

I met Mom in the lobby of the bank, told her I wasn't thirsty anymore, and waited for her to kiss Robert goodbye. In the meantime, I gazed out the large front window and watched people stroll by, laughing and shopping, with no idea that the picturesque view they saw might go away soon.

"Where to next?" Mom opened the door.

"The drugstore." I stepped into mid-morning sunlight and glanced at the old-fashioned red-and-white awning over Oak Meadows Drugs. The vintage feel of the place had me wishing I'd grown up in the town, back when poodle skirts were all the rage and innocence wasn't a thing of the past. Matt and I could have shared an ice cream float at the counter.

"What's wrong with you?" Mom frowned. "Are you going to stand there staring or are we going in?"

"In. Sorry. The pain meds must have me in a fog." She didn't need to know it was the shock of how formidable a foe Larkin Enterprises really was that had me in a stupor. Why had I thought they were small time business?

"Good morning, ladies." Seth Bridger, a sixty-something man with a head of wavy gray hair, wiped down the soda counter. "What can I get you?"

I perched on a red and chrome stool. "We're collecting signatures to keep investors from buying up Main Street."

"I'll sign twice." He grinned. "Do you think it will work?"

"The only thing that will work is if everyone stands firm against rising dollar signs and refuses to sell. I'm hoping that if the majority sign this petition, those on the fence will realize the futility in selling. At least I'm praying that's what happens."

"Five hundred thousand dollars is a lot of money to most people." He tossed the rag under the counter. "Especially to someone thinking about retirement. Still, I'd rather have someone take over this place than sell out to an investor."

"Thank you." I slid the clipboard across the counter. "Have you had weird things happening around here that might make you lean toward selling if they continued?"

"I've had graffiti, my tires flattened, and a window busted."

All things that sounded as if a gang of rowdy youths were having a bit of mischief. "Have you alerted the police?"

"Yes. Detectives Jones and Steele were here yesterday. They said a car would patrol the street at night."

It would take me a while to get used to calling Wayne Detective Jones instead of Officer Jones.

"At least I haven't found a dead body in my shop, right, Anne?" He winked. "That might set my wife over the edge and force me to sell out. I hired that boy, Rusty, to help keep an eye out and do some minor cleaning, but he hasn't seen anything yet."

So, that's where my gardener had gotten off to. I'd wondered why my lawn was getting long. Still, I wouldn't begrudge Rusty the work.

A customer entered and we said our goodbyes, heading next door to Classy Classics, the women's boutique. Nancy Caldwell stood behind the counter adding figures on an old-fashioned adding machine. She'd mentioned once that Excel spreadsheet was like speaking French to her and she'd continue to do what was tried and true.

She glanced up. "Anne Nelson, you look fabulous!"

I grinned. Nancy, with her bouffant hair and pencil skirt looked like she came out of the same era as my mother. Regardless of her personal style, though, the clothing she carried was stylish and reasonably priced, encompassing vintage and modern styles.

"Thank you." Mom patted her dress. "My daughter thinks I look old-fashioned."

"Good style is never old-fashioned. Now, what can I do for you ladies? I got a new shipment of sundresses in yesterday."

"We're here to ask you to sign this petition." I handed her the clipboard.

"Gladly. That Larkin fella is becoming a real pain in my … behind." She gave a firm nod of her head to emphasize the point. "I do a good business here, and derive a lot of satisfaction from being successful. I told him that, too, but you know what he said? He said, I'd do better in a mall. Really? I said. When I own this little slice of heaven and would have to rent space in a mall for an astronomical amount? No thank you, I said." She signed her signature with a flourish.

She made a good point I hadn't thought of. Space in a mall would be expensive.

She pointed the pen at me. "You tell that hunk of a boyfriend of yours to tell the Larkin people to stop dumping garbage across my stoop. Childish pranks will not get me to sell out."

"You aren't the only one being harassed. Seth next door said the police will do regular patrols of the street from now on. Do you mind?" I motioned toward the chair behind her desk.

"Go ahead, sit, you poor dear. I heard what happened to you." She clicked her tongue. "This has gone on long enough. We need to make a unified front and get these people to stop! A meeting. That's what we need."

That wasn't a bad idea. A town meeting where both sides could express their concerns.

"You know what else I heard?" She lowered her voice and glanced around as if we weren't the only ones in her store. "I heard that Ida Worthington has to return the money if the investors aren't able to purchase up all the shops they need. It was in the contract she signed. It doesn't do Steve Larkin much good to own a bookstore, now does it? If they have to cancel their agreement, Ida will be left with a business she doesn't want and have the hassle of selling her husband's business."

"But, she'd make more money holding out," Mom said.

"Tell her that. She doesn't see the big picture. All she sees is that homely mailman and a tropical island."

A bell jingled over the door causing us to turn. Mrs. Rogers entered, took one look at me, and turned and left. Good grief.

"That's a strange woman," Nancy said. "She buys stuff from me all the time, and I've yet to see her wear anything other than housedresses and stretchy pants."

While Mom and Nancy gossiped, I watched out the window as Mrs. Rogers ducked into the drugstore, returning moments later with a brown paper bag. Alcohol or drugs? Either one might loosen her up. I shook off the horrible thought and said a prayer of repentance. As unfriendly as the woman might be, it wasn't a reason for me to be unkind.

Rusty, broom in hand, marched down the sidewalk and started sweeping in front of the drugstore with enthusiasm. Dust flew, coating everything within reach. My guess was that Seth went along after Rusty left and recleaned.

Mid-stroke, Rusty stopped and craned his neck. He dropped the broom and took off running. I started after him, until my head reminded me that running wasn't in my near future. Instead, I stood half in the shop and half out as Rusty turned the corner down the street.

"What do you see?" Mom asked.

"Rusty took off down the street. Odd behavior, even for him."

"Let's stroll that way. Maybe we'll catch him on the way back. Thank you for your support, Nancy. I'll take a look at those new dresses when I have more time." Mom tossed a wave over her shoulder as we stepped back outside. "Looks as if someone is clearing out Rocking Reads."

Sure enough, a moving truck pulled up in front of the store. I was torn between locating Rusty or seeing what was happening next door to the bakery. Especially since Nancy had commented that the money wasn't Ida's yet. If it wasn't, then why did she feel free enough to sell off her husband's possessions?

I chose to question Ida. We walked as

fast as my pounding head would allow and stopped her from getting into her car.

She scowled. "You again? Can't you leave me alone?"

"Just a few more questions." I leaned against the car. "Selling out?"

"What does it look like? I don't need all those books. A store in Little Rock purchased them."

"I heard the money from Larkin wasn't yours yet."

"It isn't, but these books fetched a pretty penny. If the rest of you fools don't sell, I'll still come away with something. Please step away from the car. I have business to attend to." She slammed the door closed and started the engine.

I stepped away. Circumstances surrounding the woman got more interesting with each passing day. She was right. The books would bring in a lot of money. Enough for her to leave Oak Meadows and begin a new life somewhere else. Once the police solved the mystery surrounding her husband's death, she would be gone.

By lunchtime, Mom and I had one more store to visit. I stood outside Other People's Treasures and shuddered. The cluttered, dusty, dark thrift store always gave me the creeps. The owner, a little old lady named Betty Caletti reminded me of every witch picture that terrified little kids.

"Stop being a baby." Mom opened the door. "She won't hurt you."

She very well might. I followed Mom inside and stayed near the door where the sun through the window chased away the shadows.

"Are you going to look around or stand there all day," Mrs. Caletti cackled.

"Good morning, Betty." Mom set the clipboard on the cluttered counter, having to move aside a dusty plastic skull in order to do so. At least I hoped it was plastic. "We're collecting—" she began.

"I know why you're here and the answer is no." Betty straightened as much as her curved spine would let her. "I'm an old woman. This store barely pays my living expenses. That money will let me spend what's left of my life in comfort."

"But you could sell for much more than that," Mom said. "To someone who wants to keep Main Street the way it is."

"I could, but that would take time. Time I might not have."

In my opinion, the woman would probably outlive me. I wasn't too concerned about her wanting to sell. She'd most likely get the same terms as Ida. As long as we had the support of the majority, the town would be fine. "Thank you for your time." I backed from the store and back into the safety of the sunshine.

"That doesn't surprise me," Mom said. "She's got to be pushing ninety."

"Not a lot of time left to spend even five hundred thousand." A commotion at the end of the street drew my attention, reminding me horribly of something similar that happened last year.

Rusty, covered in blood, at least I thought it was blood, raced toward us. He stopped a foot away and bent over, gasping. "Dead. Alley."

"Call 911." Ignoring the hundreds of

dwarves mining for gold in my brain, I dashed in the direction Rusty pointed.

13

"Where's the body?" I asked Rusty.

He pointed to a burlap sack.

Okay, I might be drugged, but even I could tell the bag was too small to contain a human body. I gasped. What if it only contained a piece of said body? My stomach rebelled.

"Rats," Rusty said.

"Excuse me?"

"Dead rats. Here's a note." He thrust a piece of paper, covered in the same red substance he was, at me.

"Is that blood or paint?"

"Paint." He grinned. "I'm painting fire hydrants."

Wonderful. I read the note. "Sell and move out or they won't be dead next time. I will release a plague of Biblical proportions." I sighed and opened the bag.

Ten dead rats stared up with vacant eyes. In the distance, the wail of police sirens alerted me to the fact I'd jumped to conclusions. Something I should never do when Rusty was involved.

I sat on an overturned crate and waited to explain myself to the authorities. "I thought someone was dead, Rusty."

"The rats are dead." He chewed on the cuticle to his right thumb.

"Yes, they are." I glanced to the end of the alley where Matt and Wayne rushed toward us.

"Where's the body?" Matt scanned the area.

"More than one actually." I pointed to the sack. "I misunderstood. I'm sorry."

"Vermin?" Wayne frowned. "You called 911 because of a bag of dead rats?"

"There is a threatening note." I held out the paper. "Rusty cried body and I had Mom call you." I pushed to my feet. "In my defense, there was an actual body the last time he did this."

"True." Matt took my face in his hands. "How are you feeling? You aren't overdoing things, are you?"

"Trying not to." I forced a smile, doing my best to ignore the ache in my head.

He turned to Mom, who rushed into the alley through the back door of her shop. "I think Stormi needs to go home." He kissed the end of my nose with promises to stop by later, then turned to his partner. "Let's bag the rats and note and head back to the precinct."

I followed Mom into the shop and motioned for Rusty to come with us. I gave him a cupcake and sent him on his way after a lecture about what was important enough to scare someone and what wasn't. And, he had scared me.

After the last few mysteries I'd gotten involved in, I expected to find a dead body around every corner. The fact that Jim Worthington was the only one killed so far, set my nerves on edge. I was happy no one else had died, but couldn't help waiting for the other shoe to drop. It really wasn't a healthy way to live.

Mom drove me home where Mary Ann waited on the front porch. "I'll be back in a few hours," Mom said. "Get some rest."

I headed straight to the kitchen and to the notepad of notes. "We got everyone on Main Street to sign except for Mrs. Caletti. She wants to retire in style."

"It's better than selling used junk." Mary Ann plunked a pain pill and a glass of water in front of me.

I declined the pill, wanting to be able to think straight, but guzzled the water. "The thing that's strange to me is … the people who are selling don't seem to care that the property is worth twice what Larkin is paying. The majority realizes the true value and either wants to wait until some time in the future to sell or plans on working indefinitely." I stared at the pad of paper, jotting notes from the day's conversations next to each name.

"Those who aren't selling are being harassed. Silly things, like a group of kids are behind the pranks."

"Nothing vicious enough to warrant Jim's death?"

"No." I sat back in my chair. "I almost feel as if we're dealing with two different, but related, mysteries."

"As in someone wanted Jim dead and someone else wants the businesses to sell?"

"Exactly."

She sat across from me. "Which leads us right back to the jolly widow."

"And Steve Larkin is the one threatening the businesses. All we have to do now is prove it."

She grabbed a banana from a bowl in the middle of the table and peeled it. "The thing that strikes me as strange is Larkin's delivery. If the pranks against the businesses seem childish, that goes against what I've seen of the man."

I shrugged. "Make things annoying enough and everyone has a price." I glanced out the window to see Mrs. Rogers tape a sheet of paper to one neighbor's house and move to the next one.

"Take her for example. She thinks if she can get enough signatures from the neighbors, or irritates me enough, I'll up and move."

"What do you think she's saying now?"

"That I'm an evil murderer who belongs behind bars. She doesn't believe that we were only plotting to kill her on paper."

"What's our next step?"

"A sting operation? A stakeout?" It was impossible for me to watch Ida and Steve at the same time, and almost as impossible for me to delegate and let someone else watch one of them. Yet, I couldn't be in two places at once. Mom and Greta would have to watch one or the other.

Dakota! He had equipment that would come in handy. I bolted from my chair and upstairs with Mary Ann close on my heels.

"My nephew has spy equipment somewhere. See if you can find anything."

"I'll check the closet." She rummaged through boxes on the top shelf. "Uh-oh. You need to see this." She turned with a shoe box in one hand.

"What is it?" I glanced inside to see a pipe and several baggies of green stuff. "Is that pot?" Not Dakota. My heart dropped to my knees.

"It looks like it. What do you want me to do with it?"

"I'll take it. Maybe there's a good explanation." Although, I couldn't come up with a single one.

"Here we go." Mary Ann dragged a box from behind skateboard equipment. "There are cameras, listening devices, and more. Everything we need."

I couldn't think of anything other than the box in my hand which contained illegal drugs. In a trance I headed for the kitchen. My nephew wouldn't be home for three more hours. What was I supposed to do with the stuff until then?

The doorbell rang, bringing me out of my stupor. I shoved the box into Mary Ann's hands. "Hide it."

"Where? The top of the refrigerator?"

"No. That's the first place the cops will look."

"You don't even know that the cops are at the door. It could be a salesman."

I shook my head. "Matt said he was coming over here." We were going to be arrested. Dakota would go to juvie.

"For Pete's sake." She dropped the box on the kitchen table. "It looks like a pair of shoes. No one is going to look inside." She marched past me and to the front door. "Act innocent. It's my brother." She opened the door and smiled. "Yay! They brought Chinese food."

They? I peered around the corner to see Matt and Wayne carrying boxes of food. We were dead.

I grabbed the box and set it on the counter next to the toaster. If we acted cool and ignored the box, no one would notice it. I pasted on a grin and grabbed a handful of paper plates from the cupboard. "Thank you for bringing lunch."

"You're welcome." Matt wrapped his arms around my waist and nuzzled my neck. "I figured you probably hadn't put anything in your stomach other than drugs, and—"

"Drugs?" I stiffened, my gaze landing

directly on the box in front of me. "Why would you say that?"

"You are on pain medications, right?" He turned me to face him. "Are you all right?"

"I'm fine. Just a bit muddled, but I haven't taken any since this morning. I don't like how they make me feel." I made a beeline for the table. "Have a seat and Mary Ann and I will tell you what we found."

"We will?" Her eyes widened. "Are you sure?"

"Of course, silly." I gave her a stern look, trying to tell her to shut up and follow my lead. "I did promise Detective Jones, didn't I? That I would share all information pertaining to the case?"

"Oh, yes. Whew!" She sat down and flashed a grin at the men. "She did promise."

Matt crossed his arms. "What is going on?"

"That's what we're trying to find out." I opened a box of kung pao chicken. "We think we're focusing on one mystery, when in fact, there may be two."

The look on his face told me he knew I was redirecting his attention, but bless his heart, he played along. "Go on."

Wayne scooped fried rice onto his plate. "You don't think Jim's death is related to the pranks around town?"

"Maybe in a roundabout way," I said. "But the pranks aren't personal. They're directed at everyone. Jim's death, while not directed at Mom despite the fact he was found in her store, was still personal."

"Makes sense in a strange way," Matt said. "It at least gives us reason to look at the entire picture from a different angle. Still, Worthington's death started the whole battle for Main Street. There's more to his death than an investor wanting his property. You did good, Stormi." He glanced up and winked. "But now, it's probably time for you to let us handle it."

Wayne laughed. "I guess you had to say that out loud, but you know she isn't going to listen."

"You're right. I had to say it."

"Very funny, you two." I glanced at

the clock. A whole hour had passed since finding the box. I needed to get rid of them before Dakota came home. "I'm very tired. I think I'm going to lie down."

"Can I do anything?" Matt stood and helped me to my feet.

"No, thanks. I'll just go lie down on the sofa." I purposely ignored the box on the counter and shuffled from the kitchen.

Matt lowered me down and covered me with an afghan. "I need to get back to work. Will you be all right? I can have Mary Ann stay."

"That would be great. I have some research for her to do."

He kissed me, then moved his mouth to my ear. "We'll talk later about what's really going on."

My smile fled. He tweaked my nose and strolled from the room, taking Wayne out of the house with him.

"That was close." Mary Ann plopped into the chair across from me, the box of drugs and paraphenalia in her lap. "Now what?"

"We wait for Dakota to get home,

demand an explanation, and get rid of it."

"Isn't that illegal?"

"I'm not going to have my nephew go to jail." I tossed the afghan over the back of the sofa. There had to be a good reason why he had the marijuana.

For the next two hours, after trying unsuccessfully to put words to paper, Mary Ann and I watched home decorating shows. When the front door opened, we snapped to attention and turned the television off.

"Dakota?"

"Yeah?" He stepped into the living room, his eyes widening at the sight of the box on the coffee table. "Where did you get that?"

"From your room. I was looking for spy equipment." I crossed my arms, tears pricking my eyes. His guilty expression didn't bode well for his giving me an innocent explanation.

"I'm going to the kitchen to give you two some privacy," Mary Ann said. She gave Dakota a stern look on her way out.

"I might as well come clean." He tossed his backpack on a chair. "I took it as payment, sort of."

"For what? What kind of job could you possibly do that would require payment in drugs?"

"I have someone spying on someone, and in order for that someone to do it, they asked me to temporarily hold onto this."

"That's no excuse. Why would you—" My head was starting to ache again.

"Sometimes, as a detective, a man has to bend the rules a little," he said. "Want to know what I found out?"

14

"Yes." This had better be good.

He plopped on the arm of the sofa, giving me a clear look at the bottom of his shoes. "Do you know Phil Davidson?"

I nodded, unable to take my sight off the red paint ground into the design of his gym shoe tread.

"Well, since he lives next to Mrs. Worthington, I asked him to keep an eye on who comes and goes from her house. In exchange for him doing me a favor, I had to do one for him." He waved a hand toward the shoe box. "I'm supposed to take the box back to him tonight. His mom said if he didn't stop keeping the stuff at his house, she was going to toss it."

"So, you thought it would be a good

idea to keep it here?" I crossed my arms. "You do know I'm dating a police detective, right?"

"Yes, I'm not an idiot."

I hadn't thought so, but the shoe box stunt made me wonder.

"She gets a lot of visitors, but the mailman is the one who visits Mrs. Worthington the most. And," he raised his eyebrows, "she receives a lot of packages."

I shrugged. Since she was coming into money, it made sense she would be spending it. "I still don't see why you had to break the law in order to spy on her. You haven't found out anything more than what I already knew."

"You break the law all the time."

"This is not the same thing and you know it." I shoved to my feet and grabbed my purse. "Let's go. We aren't keeping that box in the house one more minute."

I explained to Mary Ann where we were going and she decided to head home and make sure Matt didn't come around until I got home. Relationship or not, I wasn't sure how much I could get him to look the other way when drugs were involved.

"You can't drive," Dakota said. "You're on pain meds."

"I haven't taken any since this morning."

"You're weaving."

"Fine. Mary Ann!"

She stopped halfway down the sidewalk. I tossed her the car keys and set the security alarm on the house. If my nephew thought I was still under the influence of medication, it didn't do my case against drug use any good if I were to drive.

"Do you want me to stay in the car?" Mary Ann asked when we pulled up in front of Mrs. Davidson's house.

"Yes," Dakota said. "Phil won't come out if he sees you." He studied me for a moment. "You either, Aunt Stormi. You're both too close to Matt."

"Then I'll wait around the corner of the house," I said. "I'm not letting you speak to a drug dealer alone. I have experience at this, remember?"

He rolled his eyes. "We aren't dealing with a gang. It's one random person who sells pot."

Pot that had to come from somewhere other than Phil Davidson. Instead of correcting my nephew, I closed my eyes, said a prayer for wisdom, and had Mary Ann drop us off out of sight of the Davidson's house with strict instructions to keep her eyes peeled. If it looked like we could be in danger, she was to call her brother right away.

While Dakota approached the front door of our target, I ducked around the corner and hid behind a juniper bush. Behind the house and to the right was a dilapidated shed that looked as if a strong wind would blow it over. An unlatched door banged to and fro, making it difficult for me to hear anything that might be happening on the front porch.

"I told you not to bring that back here."

I held my breath as Phil and Dakota marched around the house and toward the shed.

"My aunt found it and said I couldn't

keep it at the house," Dakota said.

Phil whirled. "You told her—" His gaze met mine. His mouth fell open. He snapped it closed and continued his march to the shed.

Since I'd been discovered, I stood and followed.

"My mom is going to kill me." He grabbed my arm and pulled me into a shed so full of broken furniture and boxes, there was barely enough room for the three of us to stand. "What is going on? Are you going to turn me in?"

"I should, but I have other things on my mind than this. What have you discovered about Mrs. Worthington?"

He shook his head. "Something is fishy about her and her boyfriend. Also, the last few days, no other man, except for Mr. Franklin, has visited her."

"Well, she is getting ready to move."

"No, it's more than that. She's reverting back to the same type of cowed behavior she had when her husband was still alive. I don't think everything is rosy in her world."

I glanced out the door and toward

Ida's house as Dennis Franklin carried in an armload of boxes. "We need to find out what's in those boxes."

Phil paled and shook his head. "I'm done helping you. If I can't keep my stash at your place, we don't have a deal."

"Good grief." I shoved open the door and stepped outside as Mrs. Davidson lumbered across the yard. "I'll speak to your mother, but you should really consider not selling marijuana." I was going to have to turn him in eventually, but hoped for a few more days to clear up the mystery surrounding Ida.

"What is going on here?" Mrs. Davidson crossed her arms, causing her ample bosom to strain against the buttons on her housedress. "If you're here to buy anything—"

"No, I've hired your son to do a bit of spying for me." I forced a grin.

She cocked her head. "Is that so? Well, if it's legal, I don't care what you hire him to do. Phil, I told you to get the paint out of the living room." She turned and headed back to the house.

"I'm sorry. Mom is usually more friendly, but someone turned her in about the house being in such bad shape."

"What do you mean?"

"Mom's a hoarder." He sighed. "We have thirty days to clean out the house or be evicted. She's been in a bad mood ever since she found out. That's how she discovered my stuff. She was going through my room trying to find the cord to the laptop so she could get online to find a professional organizer."

I nodded as if that made perfect sense. "Please keep me informed if you find out anything more about Ida Worthington that might shed some light on her husband's death. I'll pay you a hundred dollars if your information leads to the case being solved."

"Deal." He thrust out his hand.

I returned the shake. Noticing a red substance under his fingernails, I slid my hand free as soon as possible. I didn't know whether it was blood, paint, or something unidentifiable and wasn't going to stick around to find out. "Let's go, Dakota." I made a beeline for the road and Mary Ann.

"Are you going to tell Mom?" Dakota jogged to catch up with me.

"Probably. I just don't know when." If he were my son, I would want to know, even if it hurt. But first, I needed to find a way to tell Matt that wouldn't get my nephew into too much trouble.

"I'm dead." He climbed into the back seat and slammed the door.

As soon as we were in the car, I texted him, asking him to stop by the house at his earliest convenience. He responded that he was already there.

That didn't bode well. We rushed home to discover him sitting on the front porch, alone.

"Go to your room," I told Dakota. "I'll call you if we need you."

He nodded and slipped past Matt without saying a word.

Matt took a deep breath. "Are you ready to tell me what's going on? The two of you were stranger than normal at lunch."

I told him what Mary Ann and I had found and where we had been. "I was going to tell you, I promise, just not right now. Please don't arrest Dakota."

"I'm not going to." He resumed his seat on the porch swing and patted the cushion for me to join him. Mary Ann sat in a rocking chair across from us. "We've been watching Philip Davidson for months. We aren't interested in wasting our time with the little guys, we want the ones supplying him."

"And we just tipped him off."

"Possibly." He set the swing into motion. "We aren't dealing with anything as big as the gang a few months ago, but it's enough for us to assign an officer to the case. Jim Worthington's death takes precedence right now."

"Any more news?"

"Nope." He put his arm around my shoulders and pulled me close. "You know as much as we do. Jim was killed in the alley and dragged into your mother's shop. No why or who yet."

"Any idea who is harassing the shop owners?"

He shook his head. "No, and Larkin denies any knowledge of the pranks."

We weren't any closer than we were days ago. I snuggled into him and wondered whether I should mention the red paint on Dakota's shoes and under Phil's fingernails. Just when I'd decided it wouldn't hurt to mention it, Matt's cell phone rang.

"Detective Steele." He listened for a moment. "I'll take care of it. I'm right across the street."

"What?" I straightened.

"Mrs. Rogers is complaining because you're associating with a known drug dealer."

"How does she know that?"

"She drove by when we were parked outside Mrs. Davidson's house," Mary Ann said. "It looks like she's expanding her reach where the fliers are concerned."

Matt exhaled sharply. "I'll see if I can get her to stop distributing them." He tweaked my nose, then planted a quick kiss on my lips. "Tell Dakota he isn't in trouble this time, but if I find out he's holding anything illegal for anyone again, I will throw his behind in juvie. Can I take you out to dinner tonight?"

"I'd love that."

"Wear something nice. I'll pick you up at seven." Another quick kiss and he moved across the street and knocked on Mrs. Roger's door.

I stayed outside and watched as the old bat stepped outside and pointed in my direction. If she knew so much, she had to know I was dating Matt. What did she expect him to do? I hadn't spoken to her or stepped on her side of the street in days. Old woman or not, she needed to find someone else to aggravate.

Rusty strolled down the sidewalk, stopped and stared at Matt and Mrs. Rogers, then darted across the street and into his house two doors down from Mrs. Rogers. If anyone else had exhibited that type of behavior, I might have thought twice about it. But, considering it was Rusty, I shook it off and waited for Matt to return.

Fifteen minutes later, he strolled up the sidewalk and stopped at the bottom of the stairs. "She thinks you're watching her through her curtains as she watches television in the evenings and showers before bed."

I had no idea what to say to that.

"I told her it was probably Rusty. I'm headed over there to speak with him now. He has got to stop the Peeping Tom act."

I agreed, but sometimes the gentle giant actually discovered things of value.

15

I slathered clear lip gloss over a rose-colored lipstick as the doorbell rang downstairs. When it rang a second time, I realized none of my family was home. I grabbed my evening clutch and dashed to greet Matt.

His gaze raked over the body-hugging black dress I wore. "Wow."

I laughed. "I've worn this dress before."

"You still take my breath away." He locked the door and set the alarm for me. "Let's see if we can have a nice dinner without someone shooting at us."

"I agree." Especially since those types of nice dinners were rare for us. Either we were shot at or we ended up chasing down a suspect. It would be nice to act as a normal couple in love for once.

"Maybe you should take me out to a fancy restaurant when we aren't investigating a case."

"I can't get used to the fact you say *we* are investigating." He opened the door to my Mercedes, since I refused to climb into his truck while wearing a dress.

"Well, we are." I flashed him a grin. My man might have resigned himself to my gum-shoeing, but I didn't think he would ever like it. "Just not together."

A dimple winked in his cheek. "Whatever you say, dear." He closed my door and jogged to the driver's side. He slid behind the wheel. "I don't think Mrs. Rogers is very happy about us dating." He motioned his thumb over his shoulder.

"She isn't happy about anything I do." I still had no idea why the woman disliked me so much. It couldn't be because of my profession, could it? Romance writers were some of the nicest people I knew. We often helped newbie writers get started in the business, donated books to women's shelters and prisons. What was there not to like?

Matt drove to a fabulous steak and seafood restaurant on the banks of Oak Meadows's lake. Since he had a reservation, we were able to get a table at a window overlooking the water. We'd sat there before, only to have the window explode from a bullet aimed at me. Since I had yet to receive any threatening notes from anyone other than Mrs. Rogers, I felt safe enough to settle in and enjoy the evening. Somehow, I couldn't picture the old woman shooting anything but words.

"How did it go with telling Rusty to stop peeping in windows?" I asked after the waitress took our orders. "I've been telling him that since the first day I met him."

"He wouldn't answer his door." Matt shook his head. "If I get many more complaints, I'm going to have to arrest him."

"That won't work. He doesn't understand."

Matt reached across the table and took my hand. "I won't arrest him unless I absolutely have to. You know that."

"Let's not talk about unpleasant things." But then again, what would we talk about? We've never been the sort to spout sweet nothings. Most of our conversations consisted of whatever crime I was meddling in, Matt's concerns for my safety, and what my next move would be.

I stared into his hazel eyes, focusing on how they softened right before he kissed me or how they hardened when I did something to upset him. He never stayed mad long. Even the times I'd tried to push him away because of insecurity when I felt unworthy of such a wonderful man. He'd still come by and convince me how silly I was being. Matthew Steele was a fabulous one-of-a-kind man, and I was a very lucky woman.

"How is it going with your mother in the basement and Angela in the attic?" His thumb rubbed the back of my hand, sending my brain into areas it shouldn't go.I prided myself on holding tight to my vows, even one made in my Freshman year during a church revival. I could wonder and dream what it would be like to give into the temptation of Matthew Steele, but that was all. I'd come this far, what was another year or … when was the man going to propose?

"Lonely. Before they moved in, I wasn't even aware I was lonely. I craved and treasured my solitude."

"And then your agent told you to get out more, you stumble across a dead body, meet me, and the rest is history." He grinned.

I laughed. "That pretty much summed up the last year." I straightened as my filet mignon was set in front of me. "I just had a thought."

"Uh-oh." He winked. "That's always a dangerous thing.

"Hush. If I were to pursue a private investigator's license, would you sign off on me in a year?" My research told me I needed two years of investigative experience. With the way I was going, that wouldn't be difficult. I already had a year under my belt.

"Why?" He narrowed his eyes. "Are you thinking of stopping your writing?"

"Never." I cut into my steak, pleased

to see it was the exact shade of pink I liked. "But, if I have my license, it would make researching my novels a little easier. Not to mention that people would be coming to me with story ideas. It might be safer."

"I'm not sure where you're getting your logic from." He shook his head. "But you know I would never discourage you from doing anything you set your mind to."

"Wayne told me I would make a good cop."

"He's right." Matt sighed. "I may be a supportive boyfriend, but I can't help thinking once in a while how nice it would be if you sat at your computer all day doing nothing more dangerous than breaking the hearts of your characters."

His cell phone rang. He peered at the screen and groaned. "We've got to go."

"Now?" I stared down at the dinner I'd looked forward to devouring.

"We'll get the food to go." He raised his hand, signaling the waitress. "We've got a dead body."

I perked up. "Where?"

"Rocking Reads."

Five minutes later, we were out the door and speeding toward Main Street. Matt parked a few doors down from the shop where yellow crime scene tape was strewn across the front of the store. The large window, that once sported fancy letters of the book store name, sprinkled the sidewalk with sparkling shards of glass. Hanging out of the broken window was Phil Davidson. The bottom of his Nike's were splattered with red paint. I needed to have another talk with my nephew, and fast.

I spotted Dakota in the crowd and headed his way while Matt conversed with Wayne. Grabbing my nephew's arm, I pulled him to the side and away from the crowd. "What were the two of you up to?"

"Nothing." He yanked free. "Phil was making extra money painting for some dude."

"What dude?"

"He never said. Then, when you mentioned red paint on the alley wall, I started following him. He's the one who has been pulling all the pranks on the shop owners."

"Then how did you get paint on your shoes?"

"I stepped in it once while it was wet, I guess." He shrugged. "I was going to find out who had hired him, but now he's dead." Tears welled in his eyes. "I might be next, Aunt Stormi. If the killer finds out I'm nosing around—"

"We won't let that happen. Come with me." I marched to where Matt and Wayne studied the crime scene. "Dakota has something to say to you."

He explained what he had been up to the last few days, keeping his gaze averted from Phil's body. "I'm really scared now."

"You should be." A muscle ticked in Matt's jaw as he switched his attention to me. "Your family needs their own bodyguard, Stormi. If it isn't you in danger, it's someone else."

"Does this mean you'll assign someone to watch the house?"

He nodded. "Dakota, you aren't to go anywhere. No school, no job. You stay safely behind doors until we catch this killer. Understood?"

"Yes, sir."

"I'll take him home," I said. "Will you stop by when you're finished here?"

Matt nodded. "We'll have some questions. Take your car. I'll have Wayne drop me off."

I marched to my car without speaking. Inside, I turned to Dakota. "I guess the apple really doesn't fall far, does it?"

His shoulders slumped. "Mom is going to kill me, if the killer doesn't get to me first."

"You're going to be fine." I patted his knee. "Matt will make sure of it."

Angela met us at the front door. "Wayne called me and told me to get home." She wrapped her son in a hug as soon as he stepped inside. "Are you all right? You aren't hurt?" She glared at me over his head. "Look what you've done."

"Me?" I tossed my clutch purse on the foyer table. "I was having an innocent dinner with Matt."

"It's your fault he's so nosy!" She

guided him into the kitchen and into a chair. "Let me fix you some hot chocolate."

I sat in one of the other chairs and kicked off my heels. "I've decided to become a private investigator."

"We can be partners." A light gleamed in my nephew's eyes.

"Absolutely not." Angela clapped a hand on his shoulder. "You're going to be a doctor."

"I get dizzy at the sight of blood."

"Nonsense." She padded in hose-covered feet to the stove. "Did you know that boy you were hanging out with was a drug dealer?"

Dakota's wide-eyed gaze landed on me. "Uh, yes?"

She turned. "Did you or did you not?"

"I did. I was spying on him."

I almost told her he'd done more than spy on Phil, but the stony look on her face made me keep my mouth shut. The less I got involved in this little family spat, the better.

A bright light shined through the window, lighting up the kitchen. A sharp rap on the door alerted me to the fact we had company. I peered through the curtains, noted Nancy (Rhino) Rhinehart on the porch, and ducked.

"I know you're home, Stormi." She cupped her hands around her eyes and peered through the skinny window by the front door. "Your car is in the driveway, your lights are on in the house, and you were seen going inside. Now, open up."

"No comment!"

"We know your nephew was with tonight's victim."

I met Dakota's startled gaze. He shook his head. "He was already dead when I got there," he whispered. "I'm in a lot of trouble, aren't I?"

"No, you're not." Angela yanked open the front door, tossed a bucket of water outside and slammed the door shut on Nancy's scream. "Sorry! I didn't see you there," she called through the closed door.

Don't mess with a momma bear and her cub. I scuttled back to the kitchen. "That was awesome."

My sister whirled on me like a

badger. "Stay away from my son."

"That's kind of hard to do when you're living in my house." I crossed my arms. I wasn't the monster here. If she stayed home more, she might be able to keep a better eye on her children. I hadn't seen Cherokee in days.

"It isn't Aunt Stormi's fault." Dakota plopped into a chair. "She had no idea I was involved until she found pot in my room."

"She found what?!"

"I was holding it for Phil. Matt knows all about it. I went and saw him today and explained everything."

"You did? He didn't mention anything at dinner." Was my sweetie withholding information?

"Yeah, he said they're waiting for Phil to trip up and lead them to the person above him." He folded his arms on the table and let his head fall forward. "I guess that will never happen now."

Angela fell into a chair. "What is happening to my life?"

For crying out loud. "This isn't about you," I said. "Your son could be in danger. He's a sixteen-year-old kid involved in something much bigger than he is. Matt said he's not to leave the house for any reason."

"Good." She sniffed. "My son deserves house arrest."

"For what?" He lifted his head.

"Getting involved in something you had no business getting involved in. Text your sister and tell her to get home. I need my family around me."

"She's working until ten." He shook his head. "How do you not know that?"

"I'm taking a leave of absence from work until this is resolved." She bolted to her feet and removed the pan of boiling water from the stove. "My children need me."

Dakota rolled his eyes. "We aren't babies."

She patted his cheek. "You're never too old to need your mother."

"Look." I couldn't take any more of her late-in-life attempts at parenting. "Staying home isn't going to accomplish anything but put you behind on your bills. I'm home most of the time and can keep an eye on Dakota." Well, I was home most of the time when I was writing. When investigating? Not so much.

Angela shook her head. "No. You got him interested in all this. Now, look what happened."

"Fine. I'd rather solve Mr. Worthington's murder than babysit anyway." I planted my palms flat on the table. "And, I will solve it."

16

I sat on the front porch with Matt's arms around me. "Did you discover anything you can share with me?"

"No."

"You didn't discover anything or you can't share it?"

"I can't share it." His chest rumbled under my cheek as he laughed. "But, I'm not surprised you asked. I believe Dakota in the fact Phil was dead when he arrived. We were able to trace the 911 call to your nephew's phone. Since he's never given me reason to doubt his word before now, I tend to believe him."

I'd sat outside while they'd questioned Dakota, per Angela's request. It might be my house, but he was her son, and she hadn't wanted me there. I consoled myself with the fact that I'd probably hear all about it when my sister filled my mother in on the details when Mom returned from her date with Robert.

"Did you check to see where Ida or Steve Larkin were at the time of Phil's death? Were there any fingerprints?" I straightened and peered through the evening light at his face. "Why the bookstore? It's practically empty." Or was it? I needed to make another trip to investigate a little more thoroughly.

"Let us handle this, Stormi." He pulled me back against his chest. "Besides, I'd rather kiss than discuss the case."

"Do you think everything boils down to drugs or money? In every case I've investigated, it seems as if one or the other, sometimes both, are behind the crime."

"Yes." He sighed.

"Which one?"

"Pick one."

Really? Hmm. I gnawed my bottom lip. I just couldn't wrap my head around Jim being murdered for marijuana. A large amount of money, yes, and Ida was still the main person to profit from his death.

"I can hear the wheels turning in your head." Matt tilted my face to his and kissed me.

I wrapped my arms around his neck and climbed into his lap, grateful for the ivy vines that hid my porch from the prying eyes of the neighbors. Not that it would have stopped me from indulging in a bit of heavy petting, but I wasn't an exhibitionist. My breathing quickened as Matt's lips traveled from my lips to my neck. I made a sound deep in my throat, something primal and guttural, before pulling his lips back to mine.

A car pulled into the driveway and snapped us back to reality. I slid from his lap and watched as Mom and Robert made their way up the walk, hand-in-hand like a couple of teenagers. It was good to see her happy again. Dad's murder six years ago had done a number on the whole family. It probably played a big part in my drive to find justice for other victims.

"Is there seriously nowhere else to do

that than the front porch?" she asked.

"The house is full, and there's nothing to hide behind in the back yard." I laughed and kissed Matt again. "Besides, kissing out here makes us feel young." And, knowing we could be caught at any moment, kept us from stepping over a line I wasn't prepared to take.

"We heard about Dakota," Mom said, "and came home as soon as we finished eating." She patted Robert's cheek. "Thank you for a wonderful evening. I'll see you tomorrow." She planted a quick kiss on his cheek, sparing me the sight of my mother kissing her boyfriend on the lips. It was okay for me, and I reminded myself again how much she deserved happiness, but I still had a hard time seeing her with anyone other than my dad.

"Go on." Matt playfully slapped my behind when I stood. "I know you're dying to hear what your sister has to say." He gave me another deep kiss, then pulled away. "Goodnight." He strolled down the sidewalk, tossing a wave and a cheery hello to Mrs. Rogers, who peeked at us from her living room window.

I shook my head and followed Mom inside. The old woman across the street complained about a challenged person like Rusty peeping, and yet she did the same thing.

"Dakota doesn't know anything more than what he's already told you," Angela said, the moment Mom and I stepped into the kitchen.

"Phil isn't, wasn't, the master mind," I said, sitting at the table. "Did he give any clue as to where he got the small amount of drugs he sold?"

Dakota shrugged. "All I know is that it's a man. Phil said 'he' a lot."

"Why would he have been at the bookstore?"

"I don't know. I was following him, then decided to stop and get a coffee. When I came back out, I heard a yell and a crash. Then, I found him dead."

Someone was gutsy, killing Phil Davidson on Main Street where anyone strolling by could have seen. Not that there were many people out at nine at night. Oak Meadows tended to go to bed with the birds. The only stores open until nine were the drugstore and the coffee shop. Both within sight of Rockin' Reads. The killer had perfect timing.

"You didn't see anyone?" Mom asked.

He shook his head. "The street was dead. Oh." His face fell, then brightened. "I did see a shadow. I thought it was a trick of the light, since the streetlamp outside the bookstore flickers. But, now … maybe it was the person who killed Phil."

"A shadow and a person can be two very different things," I said, reaching for the clipboard of notes. Still, it warranted looking into. We couldn't discount anything at this point.

"I think we should go and check out the alley in the morning," Dakota said.

"Not you." I cocked my head. "You're staying here with the alarm set on the house and Sadie to protect you. I'll go investigate."

"That dog can't protect anything." Angela crossed her arms. "I'm taking the day off work. I can't take any chances something will happen to my son."

"Why would something happen to Dakota?" Cherokee dropped her purse on the table. "Did you know the front door is open?"

Mom and I glanced at each other. "I came in last." I sighed and went to set the alarm.

When I returned, Dakota was filling his sister in on what had transpired while she was at work.

"You were helping someone who sold drugs?" Her eyes widened. "That's the dumbest thing I've ever heard. Couldn't you stick your feet in the detective pool without doing something illegal?" She glanced at me. "This is all your fault."

She was so much like her mother.

"Don't be too hard on your aunt," Mom said. "The mystery bug has hit me, too. Your brother has been ordered by Matthew to stay in the safety of this house. Stormi and I will solve the case without him." She raised a hand to stop his protests. "Until you're eighteen and can make your decisions."

"Don't you care about the safety of your grandson?" Tears welled in Angela's eyes. She tended to resort to tears when Mom didn't take her side. "Don't you want him to live past the age of eighteen?"

"Don't be ridiculous. Of course I do, but I also know that kids are going to do what they want to do regardless of my wishes." Mom grinned and rubbed her hands together. "So, where do we start in the morning?"

"I'm pretty sure the police found something of significance." Angela's eyes dried miraculously. "Remember, I work at the station. I have full confidence in the ability of our police force."

Mom and I glanced at each other, then ducked our heads to hide our grins. I had confidence in Matt, and possibly Wayne, but the other two regular officers spent more time behind their desks then they did pounding the pavements. No, I've come to realize that things moved a lot faster with my help. Not always in a good way, but I tended to stir things up until something happened to solve the case.

"Dakota can still help." I ripped off the sheet of paper with the names of our suspects. "Go online tomorrow and find anything out of the ordinary about these people. Don't skip over anything."

"I can do this." He took the paper and raced upstairs.

"Go to bed!" Angela called after him. "You can do that in the morning."

"He doesn't have to go to school?" Cherokee frowned. "Maybe I'm in danger. Maybe I should stay home."

"This is your senior year." Angela took a deep breath. "You have to go to school."

"This isn't fair. He has all the fun." She flounced from the room.

"I need to get my own place," my sister moaned. "This house is a bad influence on my children."

Right. Blame it on my house. I shrugged. "I'm going to bed. See y'all in the morning."

I'd no sooner put my foot on the bottom stair than the doorbell rang.

Figuring it to be Matt, I opened the door without looking out the window and found myself propelled backward by a punch from the meaty fist of Mrs. Davidson. Before I could scramble to my feet, she grabbed the front of my shirt, yanked me up, and slammed me into the wall.

My family raced to the rescue, piling on top of us like football players after a fumble and collapsing Mrs. Davidson on top of me. I couldn't breathe. "Get. Off."

I rolled from under the pile and grabbed my Tazer from my purse. "Watch out." I zapped our late night visitor and watched as Mom and Angela tied her hands behind her with strands of crochet yarn and left her trussed up on the floor.

Mrs. Davidson glared at me, but, since she was unable to speak, I relaxed and pulled up a chair. "I understand that you are distraught," I said. "I forgive you. But, I will not hesitate to zap you again if you try to hurt me. Blink if you understand."

She blinked.

"Great. The effects of the Tazer will wear off in a few seconds and you will have an opportunity to tell me why you hit me." I rubbed my throbbing jaw, knowing that with my fair skin, I'd sport a colorful bruise by morning.

"I called Matthew," Mom said. "He's on his way."

"I wish you wouldn't have. Mrs. Davidson?"

She nodded and scooted to a sitting position. "It's your fault my son is dead. If you hadn't of come snooping around my place, he would still be alive."

"That isn't the slightest bit true. Your son was involved in dangerous activities. A life of crime doesn't pay." I glanced at the door as Matt barged in.

"Are you all right?" He knelt in front of me. Taking my face in his strong hands, he turned my head from one side to the next. "You're going to have a nice bruise in the morning."

"I'm fine. I'm not pressing charges, but I could use a couple of aspirin."

Matt transferred his attention to my assailant. "Why are you here to assault

Miss Nelson?"

Tears poured down the woman's round cheeks. "She's the last known person Phil talked to."

Not true. But I wasn't going to implicate my nephew, and I didn't know the identity of his killer.

"That doesn't give you the right to attack her." He sniffed. "How much have you had to drink?"

"One glass of wine."

"I doubt that. You reek." He helped her to her feet. "I'm going to untie you and call you a cab. You're in no shape to drive. If you make a move to attack Miss Nelson again, she has every right to defend herself. Understand?"

She eyed the Tazer in my hand and nodded. "I'm sorry."

"Apology accepted. Do you have any idea who might have killed your son?" I moved my jaw back and forth, grateful it still worked.

"No." She slumped onto the sofa. "My son was nothing more than a loveable fool. I'd been on him for months to stop peddling drugs. Nothing big, but even a baggie was too much, right? I thought for a while, he had found other work to do.”

Matt nodded.

“Before he left the house tonight, he said he had information for Miss Nelson but had to make sure he had his facts straight before talking to her.” She raised red-rimmed eyes to me. “I assumed he had made it here before being killed. I couldn’t think past that.”

“You have no idea what he was going to tell me?”

She shook her head. “Only that he mentioned you were in danger.”

17

After a sleepless night of Mrs. Davidson's warning ringing in my head, and dreams of Dad's murder over five years ago, I stood in front of Rocking Reads. If I were honest with myself, I might not have chosen to solve, and thus write, romantic true crime mysteries to cater to new readers, but it was really because of Dad's unsolved murder that kept me stepping into dangerous territory.

It wasn't that I had no faith in law enforcement, not really, but they were often overworked or a case was shadowed by something new and more violent. Dad's murder had been chalked up to a burglary gone wrong, and while I had no reason to believe otherwise, the thought of helping other people get the closure my family never got, helped keep me investigating.

I couldn't enter through the front door of the bookstore, not with crime scene tape flapping in the morning breeze. Nor could I go around to the alley until Mary Ann brought me my coffee. Well, I could, but I chose not to. My brain needed caffeine in order to function.

"You're pretty deep in thought." Mary Ann handed me my drink. "See anything the cops missed?"

I shrugged. "Not unless they didn't notice the gaping hole in the window streaked with dried blood." Why didn't someone cover up the evidence of a murder with a tarp or something? "I want to go inside. There has to be a reason why Jim Worthington, the owner, and Phil Davidson, a small-time drug peddler, were both killed in the vicinity of this shop."

"Let's go through the bakery and snag a cupcake." Mary Ann led the way into Heavenly Bakes.

What a tremendously good idea. We pushed through the door of the bakery and made a beeline for the counter.

Mom handed me a red velvet cupcake with cream cheese frosting. "Your favorite."

"Yes, it is." I took a bite and closed my hands in pleasure.

"Greta and I aren't able to help you today," she said. "We have a big order that must be done by tomorrow."

"Mary Ann and I will manage. I'll fill you in later." I stuffed the last bite in my mouth, wiped my hands on a nearby rag, and pushed open the back door. "You need to get this lock fixed."

"I know."

If she would have fixed it a few weeks ago, Jim would never have been shoved into a vat of chocolate in her store in the first place. I told Mary Ann to make a note. If Mom wasn't going to fix it, then I would.

I stepped into the alley and blinked against the sun's brightness. Jim had been killed next to the dumpster and dragged into Mom's shop. Phil had been thrown through Jim's store window. My gaze fell on where the fence had been freshly painted, covering the words in red. Paint, drugs, and murder were all related to this alley somehow.

A sheet of paper bounced and danced between the cars. I bent and retrieved it. "Get rid of smut. Run Stormi Nelson out of town." I rolled my eyes, crushed the paper into a ball, and tossed it into the dumpster. Good luck, Mrs. Rogers.

I turned and stared at the back of the line of shops. There was nothing to distinguish one from the other. While the storefronts were cheerful in their vintage style, the back was a mundane taupe color. No numbers, no names, nothing but a clean line broken by doors.

I turned again, studying the fence. Cars and dumpsters filled the space to the point where little room was left to even tell what color the fence was. At the time Jim had been killed, most likely Phil, too, there wouldn't have been many, if any, cars in the parking spots.

"Give me a boost," I told Mary Ann. "I'm going diving."

She grimaced. "At least there won't be rotten food."

That's what I was hoping. "I'm not

hopeful. I'm sure this was dumped and combed through since Jim's murder." But, I had nothing else to go on. Mary Ann bent over so I could climb on her back, then tossed me inside.

"Oh, my gosh!"

"What?" She peered over.

"Look at all these books Ida is throwing away." I held perfectly good books in my hands. They weren't first addition or even classics, so not worth a lot of money. But, they were readable and someone would find them enjoyable

"Take these. We'll donate them to the library." It was a grave sin and a huge waste to throw a perfectly good book in the trash. "Rifle through the pages first, to make sure nothing important is inside, then stack them on top of Mom's car." The morning was worth the digging if for nothing more than saving the books.

"I haven't found anything in the books," Mary Ann said.

"All right." I wiped my dusty hands on my pants. "I'm not finding anything either." I grasped the edge of the dumpster and prepared to pull myself out when my gaze fell on a cardboard box with an address label to the bookstore.

I picked up the box. The postmark was yesterday. "Why would someone be shipping anything to Rocking Reads when the store has been closed for over a week?"

"Maybe it was mailed before Jim's death?"

"No. The postmark is Oak Meadows and yesterday." Why would someone mail something when it would be easier to just have it delivered? "There's no return address."

"Here." Mary Ann held up a paper sack. "I came prepared. Drop it in here. We'll give it to Matt."

"You're so smart." The box now had my fingerprints on it, but that wouldn't be a big deal once I told Matt. "I'm getting out, now." I hooked my leg over the top. "Catch me."

"What?"

Busy with the bag and possible evidence, Mary Ann had turned away, leaving me to fend for myself. Which never went well.

I fell to the ground with enough force to move the dumpster a few inches toward the fence. I lay in the dirt and gravel, fighting to catch my breath. My gaze fell on a metal grate under the dumpster. Ignoring the pain in my hip, I stretched my arm until my fingers touched the grate.

"See if you can push the dumpster farther. I see something." I turned and planted my feet against the painted green side and shoved, ignoring the pain in my side.

Hurting and sweaty, with Mary Ann's help, the dumpster moved until I was able to grab the grate and pull it off the hole. "There's something inside." I dragged out a stained canvas bag. Now that I was on the ground, I could easily see grooves in the dirt where the dumpster had been moved before.

"Do all the dumpsters have a hole under them?" Mary Ann reached out a hand and helped me to my feet.

"I have no idea. I've never looked." I groaned and sagged against Mom's car. If I looked, I was sure I'd have a huge scrape along my side. "Why didn't you catch me?"

"My hands were full. You should have waited until I was ready."

I set the bag on Mom's trunk and loosened the drawstring. Inside was a can of red spray paint, a cigarette lighter, and a baggy with traces of dried green leaves. "Bingo." Now to find out who the bag belonged to. My guess was Phil Davidson.

Mary Ann held open the brown paper bag which was quickly filling up with evidence. "Good thing I brought a grocery bag and not a sandwich one." She grinned. "I was being optimistic."

Tires crunched along the gravel of the alley. I yanked open Mom's car door and tossed the bag onto the back seat as Dennis Franklin stopped his mail carrier car next to us.

"Good morning, ladies." His smile didn't quite reach his eyes. "What are the two of you doing back here?"

"Rescuing books from the dumpster." I crossed my arms. "Please tell Ida that just because a book doesn't carry a high price tag with collectors doesn't mean it's worthless."

"I'll be sure to tell her. I delivered some yesterday, even. She forgot to cancel some of the orders. Why are you digging in the garbage in the first place?" His dark eyes, so similar to ones a person might see on a shark, stayed glued on my face.

"Mom lost an earring. Please keep an eye out while you're delivering mail. She thinks she might have accidentally tossed it, but we haven't found it."

"I'll ask around, but something like that will be hard to find." He gave a nod, glanced toward the dumpster, and drove away.

"I thought he was going to blind us with those shoes," Mary Ann said. "Did you notice them? Fluorescent lime green. Wow."

"I was too busy trying to keep him from seeing what we had in the back seat." I gathered up our evidence and hurried into the bakery. I could shove everything into one of Mom's large cake boxes and no one would be the wiser when I walked to my car.

"Why are you limping?" Mom frowned, glancing up from where she put candied rose petals onto a cupcake.

"I fell out of the dumpster. If Dennis Franklin asks, you haven't found your earring."

"I'm not even going to ask," she said.

"That's probably best," Greta added coming from the front of the store. "If we don't know, then we're innocent if questioned."

I shook my head and squeezed everything, except the books and the bookstore's latest delivery, into a cake box. "See you at home." I motioned for Mary Ann to follow me out front. We climbed into my car and hurried to the police station.

Angela glanced up from her desk as we rushed inside and frowned. Just once, I'd like for my older sister to be happy to see me. "What now?"

"I thought you were staying home with Dakota?" I propped the box on my hip.

"He didn't want me to."

She probably blamed me somehow for that, too. "Is Matt around?"

She punched a button on her desk, informed him I was here, as if she were alerting him to a horrible plague, then motioned me back.

"Thank you." I hurried down the hall, Mary Ann on my heels.

"Hey, gorgeous." Matt stepped from a conference room. Behind him, Michael Barker beamed at Mary Ann. Matt glanced from him to his sister and frowned.

"Hush," I whispered. "They like each other. Do you have a minute?"

"A quick one." He glared over his shoulder at Barker, then ushered me into his office. "Did you bring a cake?"

"No." I explained what had transpired in the alley and set the box on his desk. "It might be nothing, but we thought it worth looking into."

"Good work." He leaned against his desk. "Sweetheart, I've been thinking of what you asked in regards to me sponsoring you for a private investigator's license."

"And?" Please don't say no.

"I've been talking to some people and everyone agrees that it would be a conflict of interest. I'm going to have Wayne do it."

My hopes fell. "He doesn't like me."

"Sure he does." Matt cupped my cheek. "He just doesn't always agree with how you get your information. But … he is a stickler for the rules. Keep a log of everything you do. It will help." He brushed his lips against mine. "I'll stop by later and let you know what we find out about this stuff."

I nodded. "Okay. Mary Ann and I will be making a stop at the library before heading home." Where, hopefully, Dakota had found some interesting information on our suspects.

"Please let me know if my son is not at home," Angela said as we passed her desk. "I'm really counting on you to respect my wishes in this regard."

"Definitely." I tossed her a wave. "Keep your ears and eyes open."

She sighed. "You only put up with me for what information I might discover."

"Of course." I went outside and leaned against the car to wait for Mary Ann.

Down the street, Ida pulled in front of Rocking Reads. Without a glance to see whether anyone was watching, she ducked under the crime scene tape and into the building.

18

I waved for Mary Ann to hurry and took off after Ida. With a glance in both directions first, I followed the woman into the dark recesses of the store. She wasn't anywhere in sight, and I couldn't help but think of every B-horror movie where the Too-Stupid-To-Live heroine follows the killer into a dark building.

Mary Ann rushed into the building and barreled into me. I shrieked and turned, ready to fight.

"Don't do that." I put down my fists. "You scared me."

"What are we doing in here?"

"I saw Ida come in. Shush."

A muffled thud came from across the room, sending me and Mary Ann into a quick duck behind the counter. With the shelves empty of books, magazines, and anything to do with reading, the room echoed like a cave.

"Stay close and stay quiet." Staying low, I used the bookshelves as cover and I worked my way toward the small room at the back of the shop.

A melody rang out, then Ida's voice answering it. I clapped a hand over my mouth to keep from laughing at the tune that was reminiscent of a strip tease with a feathered boa.

"I'm looking for it, darling," Ida said. "Jim might have stashed it somewhere else. I know it isn't likely, but—Oh, all right." She hung up and muttered something about men and their stubborn ways and how she should go off and leave his fat rear end here while she went to the Bahamas.

I glanced at Mary Ann. So, everything wasn't rosy in widowhood.

Ida headed in our direction, sending me and Mary Ann scrambling for cover in the tiny bathroom. We left the door open enough to press our faces to the opening and be able to peer into the main part of the store.

Sweet little Ida cursed enough to set the place on fire. Whatever she looked for amongst the dirt and left behind boxes was eluding her. She sighed and plopped in a cloud of dust on top of the cashier's counter.

"This is a waste of time," she said, staring at the floor. "We have enough money without finding Jim's stupid retirement fund. I'd heard him grumble plenty of times about how poor we were going to be when he retired. I've had enough. I'm dirty, tired, and cranky. I need ice cream." She hopped down and practically ran from the shop.

"We'd better go, too." I stepped out of the bathroom.

It wasn't hard to determine that the person Ida had spoken to on the phone was Dennis Franklin. Nor was it hard to see that the man wasn't satisfied with selling the store property and the contents of the shop. Of course, Ida didn't receive a penny unless the other shop owners on Main Street agreed to sell. It was a big gamble for Larkin Enterprises and anyone else involved.

Enough to commit murder for? I thought so.

"Now what?" Mary Ann said. "The library?"

"Yes, and then Larkin Enterprises." I hoped to catch Steve coming or going and tail him for the rest of the day. Something had to break on this case soon.

We dropped the discarded books from the dumpster off at the library and drove to Little Rock where we parked in front of a four-story modern building housing Larkin Enterprises. With fast food bags of tacos and tall cups of diet soda, Mary Ann and I were ready to put in some hours waiting for Steve to make an appearance.

I called Dakota, who mourned the fact that no one on my suspect list ever seemed to do anything out of the ordinary. In my nephew's opinion, the citizens of our fair town had very boring backgrounds.

Mary Ann and I lasted a little over an hour before my bladder screamed for release. "Why hasn't he left for lunch? Doesn't the man eat?"

"Maybe he ordered takeout?" Mary Ann squirmed in the passenger seat. "I've got to use the restroom. His office is on the top floor. We could probably go to the lobby without being seen by him."

"Sounds like a plan." We shoved open our doors and rushed into the building.

Glossy marble floors greeted us. A cherry wood circular desk sat in the center of the foyer. A very pretty, very young woman, pasted on a smile and greeted us. Her smile fell as fast as a theater curtain torn loose from its ropes when we asked to use the restroom.

"Our facilities are for clients only," she said.

"We're here to see Steve Larkin."

Her smile returned. "Fourth floor. I'll let his receptionist know you're coming. Feel free to use the ladies room on that floor." She motioned us toward glass-walled elevators.

"Great," Mary Ann hissed in my ear. "I hope you have a good story for us being here."

"I'll think of something." I dragged her to the elevator and did my best not to do the potty dance where everyone could see us as we ascended.

The fourth floor looked much the same as the lobby, although on a smaller scale. Once you got past the receptionist desk, doors lined a hall carpeted in plush gray.

"I'm sorry to tell you that Mr. Larkin is not in yet," the receptionist said. "I tried to tell Alicia, but she said you had already entered the elevator."

I pretended to look disappointed. "I'm sorry to hear that. May we use your restroom, then possibly make an appointment? We had a long drive."

"Absolutely." She waved a well-manicured hand toward a door that said "Ladies".

"Brilliant," Mary Ann said the moment we stepped through the door. "But, you'd better come up with a reason for an appointment."

"I'll just say I've changed my mind and will call him when I decide if I want to meet or not." I slammed the stall door closed, and did my business, much to my body's relief.

We washed our hands and breezed past the receptionist desk with promises to call Mr. Larkin later. As we descended in the elevator, I glanced over and saw Steve and Ida in the elevator going up. Their eyes widened before Steve held his hand to his ear in the international signal for me to call him. I nodded.

I wouldn't call him, but suspected I'd receive a call before the day was over. I'd have to come up with a good reason for being in Little Rock at his building.

"Why do you think Ida is meeting with Larkin?" Mary Ann held the door open for me.

I stepped into the afternoon sunshine. "Do you think he's convinced more of the shop owners to sell?" Maybe it was time to pay another visit to the Main Street shops.

Mary Ann pushed me behind a tree. "There's Thomas."

I peered around her as Larkin's hired hand got behind the wheel of a silver

Dodge Charger. "Let's go." I grabbed her hand and we raced for my car. I prayed he wouldn't get too far ahead.

"We lost him." I glanced through the front windshield of my car.

"No, there." Mary Ann pointed. "He's getting on the freeway. Do you think he's headed back to Oak Meadows?"

"That's a very good guess." I pulled into the turning lane, being careful to keep two cars between us and Thomas. "I bet he's headed there to see what we're up to." It wouldn't have taken long for Steve to question his receptionist about our visit and phone his friend.

"You know?" Mary Ann settled back in her seat. "Until now, I really didn't see how this latest case could be dangerous."

"Excuse me?" I cut her a sideways glance. "Did you forget about Jim and Phil?"

She shook her head. "I guess what I mean to say is that I didn't see how it could be dangerous to us. I leaned on the side of Ida being the killer, and didn't see how she would consider us a threat." She emphasized us. "But now Thomas looks mean enough to bite the head off a rattle snake.

"Just about anyone could be a threat." I swerved around a slow-moving vehicle. Now, there was only one car between us and Thomas. "Did you forget about the sweet little librarian who wanted to kill me if I didn't write the next story fast enough to suit her? What about Rusty's mother? She didn't look too dangerous, either, but she almost killed my entire family."

"Never mind." She sighed. "I figured all the danger would be aimed toward getting the other shop owners to sell. But, if Larkin finds out we're spying on him … well, we could be next, Stormi. If we aren't murdered, my brother will kill us."

"Your brother has resigned himself to the fact," I slowed my speed and let another car slip in between us and Thomas, "that I'm getting my private investigator's license and plan on continuing to solve cases and write about them. If I get my license, there are more avenues available to me."

"Why don't you see if you can tag along on all his calls like that author on that television show?"

I shook my head. "I love your brother, but working with him all day would drive us both crazy. He is going to Oak Meadows!"

Thomas exited the freeway. I followed at a safe distance as he took the winding access road from the freeway into town.

He slammed on his brakes.

I screamed and did the same. My car swerved toward the ditch. Only quick thinking and a slam on the brakes kept us from going into the ditch.

Thomas opened his car door and exited. The hard look on his face had me pressing the lock button on my car.

"Get out." He rapped on the window.

"Not a chance."

"I can't talk to you if you're in the car," he said. "Mr. Larkin wants me to talk to you."

"You'll have to speak through the glass, because I'm not getting out."

"Will you at least follow me to the

coffee shop?”

“Yes.”

He stormed back to his car.

I glanced at Mary Ann. “What is going on? If he wanted to talk, why stop in the middle of the street? He could have waited until we stopped somewhere.”

“He isn’t the brightest bulb in the store.” She shrugged.

We followed him to the parking spots in front of Delicious Aroma. “Be ready to call 911 if he gets aggressive,” I told Mary Ann.

I stepped onto the pavement and waited for Thomas to approach us. “Did you know we were following you?”

“No. I would have stopped before driving all this way if I did. I did stop as soon as I noticed you. My boss lost your number. I tried to catch you before you left. Why were you at his office? Have you reconsidered selling?”

I didn’t think the man could talk this much. I shook my head. “That’s why you came all the way out here? Why didn’t you call my mother’s shop and ask her?” I tried to see a light of intelligence in his eyes, I really did. But, I failed.

"Mr. Larkin didn't tell me to. He said to find out what you wanted."

"I didn't want anything, Thomas. I only wanted to use the restroom and that was the closest place to go. I had to make up an excuse or they wouldn't let us in."

"Oh." He nodded. "Okay." He jogged back to his car and left.

I laughed and motioned for Mary Ann to get out of my car. "Rusty might be smarter than that man. I told him we were only there to use the restroom, he said okay, and left. All he needed to do was find out what we wanted."

Our conversation left me more confused than ever. Except for the fact that Thomas seemed likely to do whatever Larkin told him without asking questions or thinking twice, I'd have a hard time picturing the man as a killer. But, acting without a second thought could make him very dangerous. Either that, or he was as good at spinning a tall tale as I was.

19

My cell phone rang a few minutes after Thomas left us. "Hello?"

"Is this Miss Nelson? This is Steve Larkin."

I leaned against the hood of my car. "Yes, this is me."

"I'm sorry I missed you earlier. Thomas said you came in to use the, uh, restroom? I hope he didn't confuse your purpose here."

"That's about right. My assistant and I were doing some research and the young lady in the main lobby said we needed an appointment." I closed my eyes, hoping he'd buy the poor excuse.

"A pity. I was hoping you had reconsidered my offer. I'm willing to increase the price to seven hundred thousand."

Wow, I mouthed to Mary Ann. I shook my head when she asked what. "That is a significant increase. Is that what Ida Worthington was visiting you for?"

He chuckled. "I have no need to increase her offer, Miss Nelson. She's already signed an agreement. Please don't let others know of the amount I am offering you."

"I wouldn't dream of it, but I cannot make a decision without speaking to my partner. I'll be in touch." I hung up and told Mary Ann of his dollar amount.

"If we weren't concerned about his mall ruining our small town, that would be enough for you to live the idle lifestyle for a good long while," she said. She tapped her finger against her lips. "Why not offer him something else?"

"Like?"

"There's a big plot of land for sale between here and Harrisburg. It isn't good for farming, and the owner died without leaving an heir. The state would probably be happy to get rid of it. Why isn't Larkin looking there?"

That was a very good question. After the recession, there was a lot of land selling for very reasonable prices. Why was Larkin so bent on grabbing up the center of Oak Meadows and spending the exorbitant amount of cash it would take to demolish and rebuild?

I texted Matt. "Have you checked into why Larkin really wants Main Street?"

"Explain." Matt never was one for long texts.

"There is other land for sale. Why does he want this area so badly?"

"Good point. Will look into it. Luv ya."

I stared across the street, my eyes focused on nothing, and willed my brain to dig something out of nothing. Movement caused me to straighten. The dear Mrs. Rogers was handing out fliers again.

"That woman." Mary Ann sighed. "Want me to tell her to stop?"

I started to say yes, but then noticed how she stopped and talked to everyone. What if she were able to get information out of them that me, as a nosy writer, couldn't? "Does she like you?"

"I think so. She said she feels sorry for me losing my teaching job and having to work for someone like you. I didn't tell her it was my choice." She grinned. "What do you want me to do?"

"See if you can find out anything from her. I'll wait for you in the coffee shop."

Mary Ann strolled across the street, stopping first at the drugstore Mrs. Rogers had just left. I pushed through the doors of Heavenly Aroma. I met Tyler's gaze, then headed to the corner table where Norma sat.

"Are you here every day?" I sat across from her.

"Hello, to you, too. And yes. My office feels claustrophic, so I bring whatever needs my attention out here. How's the case going?"

"It's not." I crossed my arms on the table. "I've found little evidence of why Jim was killed or why Larkin wants this land so bad. Your, uh, friends, wouldn't have heard anything, would they?"

"If you mean my friends who are still plying their trade, then no. I haven't spoken to any of them in a while. Being a business owner takes up all my time." She tugged the hem of her short skirt over long legs. "But, I guess I can give a few of them a call. Is this about Larkin?"

I nodded.

"Then, I need to call a few of the higher class ones. I can't see him picking up a girl off the streets."

"I know it's a long shot, but maybe a little pillow talk will fill in some blanks."

"I could do some flirting. Try to finagle a dinner invitation out of the man."

"You'd do that?"

"Sure." She shrugged. "It wouldn't go any further than dinner, but what's the harm? I will insist on a very expensive restaurant."

I jumped up and gave her a hug. "Thank you! How are you going to manage?"

She gave a secretive smile. "I have my ways. The poor thing is already smitten with me. He's in here at least once a day and manages to find some excuse to come talk to me. I've been turning him down, since I'm not ready for a relationship, but I can give him a call. I'll let you know in the morning what I find out."

"Be careful. We don't know that he isn't the one who killed Jim." I took my drink from Tyler and settled back in my seat.

"I'll be fine. I'll have a sweet little friend strapped to my thigh."

"You are the toughest girl I've ever met." She really was. How many ex-prostitutes went into business for themselves, tried to get other women off the streets, strapped a gun to their leg, and still managed to look like every man's dream at the age of thirty-five?

"You carry, don't you?"

I patted my purse. "A glock and a Tazer. Both pink."

Her eyes twinkled. "Mine is a sexy red."

I opened my mouth to make a smart remark, but closed it when Mary Ann breezed through the door. She made a beeline for us, waved at Tyler, and plopped into a seat. "That woman really hates you."

"I hope you found information I didn't know." It hurt my feelings to know someone disliked me enough to try and run me out of town, but a girl couldn't have everyone like her.

"I think so." She took a deep breath. "Mrs. Rogers is handing out two fliers. One to run you out of town and another to run off Steve Larkin. Now," she raised her hand to halt any questions, "the reason she wants Larkin gone is the same reason everyone else does. No one wants the crowds and pollution that a mall will bring. She said she moved here for the small town feel."

Tyler brought her a coffee. "You ladies want a sandwich or something?"

I nodded, handed him ten dollars, and turned back to Mary Ann. "We know that."

"Well, I asked her why she thought Larkin didn't want to buy land cheaper somewhere else, and she said it was because he doesn't want the competition that Main Street brings when tourists flock here. I mean, look outside. For a sleepy town, we have a lot of sidewalk traffic. Even more so when the snows come."

"She's finding this out by talking to shop owners?" Maybe we needed to convince her to help us find Jim's killer.

"Yes." She twirled her cup on the table. "And, I asked her what she thought of Jim's death while she was in a talkative mood. She is convinced Ida did it. It seems the two of them were in a book club together until Mrs. Rogers found out how Ida filled her afternoons. Ida had strongly hinted at how she wouldn't shed a tear if her husband died."

I still didn't see how little Ida could have gotten her dead husband from the alley to Mom's shop. "What else?" I wrapped my lips around my straw.

"The pranks are continuing. The drugstore had the lock on the back door smashed, the clothing boutique had a break in. Nothing was missing, but all the clothes were scattered. Even the bank has been graffitted. I don't see Ida behind this type of stuff."

"Me either." And the continuing pranks would keep the police department too busy to dig as deeply into Jim's death as they needed to. Or give them enough time to investigate Larkin. "You were great, Mary Ann."

She grinned. "It pays to have people like you."

"She'll like me once she knows me better."

"I doubt it." She dodged the napkin I wadded up and threw at her. "What do you want to do now?"

"I want to visit Mrs. Davidson. She mentioned that she thought Phil had started making money in a way that wasn't selling drugs. We can stop by the bakery and take her some cupcakes." I turned to Norma. "Thank you. Please let me know how your dinner goes."

"I will." She scooted back to the table and transferred her attention back to her work.

Coffee and sandwich in hand, Mary Ann and I jogged across the street and into Mom's bakery. I ordered six carrot cake cupcakes and leaned against the counter eating while Mom packed them. As she worked, I filled her in on the morning's happenings.

"I finally got the lock fixed on the back door," she said. "When we got in this morning, there were muddy footprints from the back door to the front. Nothing missing, just the dirt. That reminded me to call the locksmith."

With a box of cupcakes balanced precariously in my lap, we drove to Mrs. Davidson's house. I'd gotten so used to seeing Mr. Franklin's mail truck outside Ida's house, I barely spared it a glance. Instead, I gave him a nod as he headed for her front door and I marched up the walk to Mrs. Davidson's.

When she answered the door, she once again led us to seats on the front porch. I'd met the mother of a hoarder a few months ago, and Mrs. Davidson showed all the signs of being one. I handed her the cupcakes. "I hope these help you feel better."

"Thank you, but I know you didn't come out here to bring me cake." She fixed her red-rimmed gaze on me.

"No, ma'am. I was thinking about something you said the other evening at my house. Something about Phil making his money?"

"Yes. I apologize again for hitting you. The bruise seems to have faded nicely."

"With the help of makeup." I smiled to take the sting out of my words.

"Phil had been leaving every evening, rather than meeting people in the road who stayed in their cars. He'd leave and come home with cash. Never did tell me who he was working for, but I've got my suspicions. Betty Caletti told me last week about the harassments they've been getting in town. Every one of them coincided with a night my boy was gone." She shook her head.

"The pranks have continued, Mrs. Davidson."

"Well, then, whoever hired my son, wasted no time replacing him, did they?" She heaved to her feet, wiping her eyes with a sodden Kleenex. "I'm tired. Thanks again for the cake." She went in the house and left us sitting there.

"Who hired Phil?" Mary Ann asked.

"Steve Larkin is my guess." He doesn't know the residents of my town very well. We tended to dig in our heels when met with opposition. While a few shop owners might cave under the offer of a lot of cash or the worry of harassment, most would refuse to budge out of sheer stubbornness.

Loud voices rose from the direction of Ida's house. I stood and craned my neck to see over the untrimmed rose bushes surrounding Mrs. Davidson's porch.

Dennis Franklin, open shirt flapping around a large belly covered with a white tee shirt, bolted out the front door. A terracotta vase followed, narrowly missing his head.

"It's my money, Dennis! You can't tell me what to do with it." Ida, hands on her hips, stepped onto the porch as Dennis fled down the steps.

"You've no sense, woman." He turned. "You're wasting our future."

"My future! Remember that. You're

only along for the ride."

"We'll see about that, dearie." He shrugged into his shirt and marched to his truck, muttering, "I've stuck my neck out for you."

20

This was an encouraging morning. I grinned at Mary Ann and sprinted for my car. "Let's follow our dear postman for an hour or so. This late in the day, his shift must be about over."

"If Ida is our killer," Mary Ann said, clicking her seatbelt across her, "then Mr. Franklin might want to consider being careful of what he says. The little widow isn't as meek as we thought she was."

"True, but I don't think she's behind the pranks." I still thought the two were separate; Jim's death and the harassment of the shop owners. "Also, if she did kill Jim, I doubt Dennis is too worried about it. He's most likely her accomplice and can turn her in."

We followed Dennis to the post office where he traded his mail truck for a battered tan Toyota. Across one side of the small truck were the words "Bad Guy" painted in a green childish scrawl.

"Now, who do we know that would call someone a bad guy?" I asked. "My guess is we need to talk to Rusty."

"He does see more than he should."

Dennis pulled out of the lot behind the post office and headed to a mobile home park on the outskirts of town. He parked in front of a dilapidated double-wide in need of fresh paint.

"No wonder the man is looking for a windfall." I entered the park and turned around in a large cul-de-sac at the end. Stopping one trailer away from the one Dennis entered, I cut the engine.

We hadn't sat there for more than fifteen minutes before I saw Rusty skulking in and out of the trailers. Since he carried a hoe, I assumed he had picked up a job as gardener for the park. I opened my door. "Stay here and keep an eye on Dennis, okay?" I told Mary Ann. "Text me if he comes out. I'm going to ask our local Peeping Tom a few questions."

I ducked behind a pink trailer and hissed Rusty's name.

He jumped two feet and doubled up the fist not wrapped around the garden tool. "You scared me."

"I'm sorry. I want to talk to you."

"I'm not peeping. I'm working."

"I can see that. I won't bother you long." I made sure Dennis couldn't see me if he glanced out his window. "Did you paint the words 'Bad Guy' on the mailman's truck?"

"Yes. It's true."

"Why is it true?"

"He's bad."

I tried not to appear frustrated. Any sign that Rusty wasn't making any sense, he'd clam up and run away. "How is he bad?"

"Mrs. Worthington is married," Rusty whispered. "He kisses her."

So did a lot of men, but I let that fact lie. "Anything else?"

"He snoops around town at night." Rusty frowned.

If I couldn't get Rusty to expand on his words, we'd be there all day. "I know you have to get back to work, so why don't you tell me everything you know so I don't have to keep asking questions?"

"Everything?"

"Only about Mr. Franklin."

"He yells at me. Once, I saw him yell at Mrs. Rogers. She doesn't like me." He frowned.

"That's okay. She doesn't like me either." It took another fifteen minutes before I realized that other than Dennis messing around with Mrs. Worthington and snooping around town after dark, Rusty didn't know anything of value about the man. Rusty promised to mow my grass tomorrow and lumbered off, shaking his head and mumbling.

I behaved pretty much the same way as I headed back to my car. A mere second after sliding into the seat, Dennis stepped out of his trailer wearing what could only be described as his "party clothes". A red and black western style shirt with black jeans. His graying hair was slicked back from his face. I wondered if Ida knew her man was stepping out on her.

"I bet he's going to that new honky-tonk bar on the east side," Mary Ann said. "We should go, too."

I glanced down at my jeans and tee shirt. "I'm not really dressed for going out."

"Sure you are. Jeans are the perfect wear. All you need is some makeup, and I have some in my purse."

I groaned and texted Matt as to where we would be, then sat back and let Mary Ann paint my face. "If he isn't at the honky-tonk, we wasted our opportunity to follow him."

"He'll be there. Look up." She slathered mascara on my bottom lashes. "A dab of rose-colored lip gloss and you're gorgeous. Even in jeans and a plain black tee shirt. Sometimes, you make me so mad."

"I'm built like a stick. You have the curves men like and big eyes that make them drool."

"I do, don't I?" She grinned. "We're different kinds of beautiful. Now, drive, Red. We've a party to go to. Remember, though … if Dennis sees us, you're only there as my wing man. Everyone in town knows you're dating Matt."

"Got it. I'm there to support you as you find a date." Good grief. I'd never been the bar-hopping type. I had no idea how to act once we got there. I went straight from a nerd in high school to a nerd in college. I'd never considered myself pretty or desirable until I saw myself through Matt's eyes. Maybe I could fade into the background and let Mary Ann do whatever it was she was going to do.

I started the car and followed her directions to a sprawling wood building on the town's border. A big neon sign, waiting for night so it could glow in all its glory, stated simply 'Roy's.' "We're too early," I said.

"No, this place opens at ten a.m. They serve great burgers."

I stared at her. "How do you know all this?"

"Michael brought me here the—" Her eyes widened. "I didn't mention we'd gone on a date, did I?"

"You did not. I thought we were best

friends. That's something a person normally tells their best friend."

She shrugged. "I didn't want to say anything until I knew where our relationship was going."

"And?" I shoved open my door.

"I really like him, and I think he feels the same way about me." She flashed a grin and got out of the car. She stood and stared at the building. "I have got to be the luckiest literary assistant in the world. How many of them get to step out of the office and do the things I get to?"

"Their lives might be boring, but they're a lot safer." I linked my arm in hers, already forgiving her for her secret regarding Michael, and strolled toward the barn-like doors of Roy's.

Loud country music from overhead speakers assaulted our ears the moment we stepped inside. A stage sat against the far wall and a polished mahogany bar took up the other end. A mirrored wall behind the bar reflected liquor bottles in a rainbow of colors and dim lighting.

Dennis Franklin bellied up to the bar, a bottle of beer in his hand as he surveyed the few people at the scattered round tables. In the center of the bar was a good-sized dance floor. No one danced that early in the day. Besides Dennis, two other men drank at the bar. Five of the tables were occupied, two by families. All were enjoying an early dinner.

I inhaled the delicious aroma of barbecue. "I'm starving." I dragged Mary Ann to a table. "Let's eat. We can spy with sauce-covered ribs in our hands."

"This place will be hopping in another hour or two," she said, sitting at a barrel-shaped chair at a table next to the dance floor. "You should text my brother to meet us here when they get off work. I'll do the same with Michael. We can keep an eye on our prey for now and have fun later."

"That's the best thing I've heard all day." I chose a chair with a clear view of Dennis and sent Matt a text. He replied, saying he would meet us in half an hour and to order food for him. Maybe I could get him to dance later.

The waitress, a big chested, skinny waisted woman in her mid-thirties, sidled up to our table to take our orders. We ordered four plates of ribs and fries, as Dennis called for his second beer.

"Hey, Angel!" Dennis rotated on his chair as the waitress sashayed past. "You ready to run off with me yet?"

"You rich yet?" She tossed back as she pushed through swinging doors to the kitchen.

"Pretty much." He grinned and turned back to the main part of the room.

"It doesn't look as if he plans on taking Ida with him once he gets his hands on her money," I said.

"Should we warn her?"

"I don't know. Isn't squealing on a cheating boyfriend something friends do? I doubt she considers us her friends."

"Call your sister. Let's see how far Dennis will go if flirted with. I'd suggest Norma, but you said she's going out with Larkin tonight. Maybe Angela can get the mailman drunk enough to spill his secrets."

"Girl, you're on a roll today with the good ideas." I texted Angela, letting her know what we needed her to do. She replied that she'd be there in fifteen minutes. She had just the dress in her car and would put it on after she clocked out of work.

Of course she could be ready for a night out on a moment's notice. Not to mention that her work clothes were skimpier than anything I owned. If I wanted to look sexy, but by today's standards, I usually borrowed something of hers.

Angela beat Matt to the honky-tonk and made a beeline for the bar. It only took Dennis seconds to move to a stool at her side. She turned, propping her elbows on the bar's surface, and jutting her endowed chest forward. My sister oozed sleaze and class all at the same time. If she weren't careful, she'd be wiping Dennis's drool off her arm. I fished my cell phone from my purse and snapped a few pictures.

"She should be in the movies," Mary Ann said, propping her chin in her hand. "There's no way I could pretend to be interested in someone like Dennis Franklin. To watch her, you'd think she thought he was the handsomest man in the state."

"I'm just glad she agreed to do it."

"What did you offer her?"

"Fifty bucks."

Mary Ann laughed, the sound rising above the music and drawing Angela's attention. She frowned and shook her head, not wanting us to take Dennis's focus off her, no doubt.

Matt and Michael, with a tag-a-long Wayne Jones, waltzed into the building and straight for our table. Matt leaned down and greeted me with a kiss. "Wayne came along when we heard your sister was going to be here, but she looks occupied."

"She's working." I smiled. "Pull up an extra chair and watch her at her best."

"Working how?" Wayne asked.

"Digging information out of a drunken Dennis." I explained the man's earlier fight with Ida and his comments about money. "Angela can get a man to say anything."

"Seeing her in that red dress makes me want to spill my secrets," Wayne said.

Matt and Michael wisely kept their thoughts to themselves. I raised my hand to attract the attention of Angel and asked her to add another order of ribs to our bill. I wasn't sure what my sister would want if she decided to join us, but it would most likely be a salad. A plate of ribs and fries would not allow her to wear dresses like the slinky thing she wore now. I sighed and reached for the glass of tea our waitress had plunked in front of me.

"Don't look so sad," Matt said, his lips close to my ear. "You're twice as sexy even in overalls."

I playfully punched his arm. "I don't wear overalls."

"Maybe not, but you'd look gorgeous in them."

My man always knew what to say.

Angela pushed away from the bar, caressed Dennis's cheek, and tossed a quick glance my way before heading for the restroom. I dashed after her.

21

"**W**ell?" I blurted the moment I stepped through the door. "You're amazing out there. You should be in the movies. You have the poor fool eating out of your hand." I looked under each of the stalls to make sure we were alone.

"It isn't hard." Angela touched up her crimson lipstick. "The idiot can't resist a pretty face or a loose woman." She grinned and scrubbed a dot of lipstick off her teeth. "You could just as easily have gotten him to talk if you dressed like a woman instead of a teenage boy."

"I dress as a woman when the situation calls for it." Like when I'm on a date with Matt or attending a conference. Dressing like a woman didn't mean looking like I charged on the street corner. Still, I didn't want to fight with my sister. Her fashion style came in handy in situations such as the one we were in. "Besides, he knows I like digging up information. He'd never trust me. So, what did you find out?"

"He's definitely after Ida for the money she might come into." She faced me and leaned against the sink. "He's worried that the offer will fall through and he is trying to come up with other ways to make a chunk of money." A shadow passed over her eyes. "You need to warn her to get rid of him. I'm afraid he might harm her to get his hands on her money. Did you know that Jim actually did have a life insurance policy? Ida found papers to the fact in the bookstore. I think Dennis is after that money."

"He'd have to marry her, then kill her." My heart stopped. We'd located Jim's killer. All we had to do now was prove it. "Stop talking to him. Come sit with us. No information is worth your safety, and Wayne came to spend time with you. Impress him with this new information."

Her face lit up. "He did?"

I nodded. "How will you get rid of Dennis?"

She tapped sculpted fingernails against the porcelain sink. Tap tap tap. I shot out my hand and stopped her.

"Well, I can slip him something to make him go to sleep. Then, when he appears to be too drunk, the bartender will call him a cab."

"Isn't that against the law?" Who was this woman?

"He's a possible murderer, Stormi." She looked at me as if I'd grown another head. "Do we care?"

"I guess not, but there are three law enforcement officers at our table who might think otherwise. You can't say a word about drugging him." I chewed my bottom lip. I'd tell Matt after he took me home. He might be mad, but surely he would see the reasoning in Angela's plan.

"Go back to the table, scaredy-cat. That way, you aren't a part of this." She stared at herself in the mirror and tugged the neckline of her dress lower.

"Thanks. Don't give him too much. We don't want him dead." I pushed open the door and joined the others.

Angela followed a few seconds later, leaned over Dennis, giving him a close-up look of her cleavage, and subtly dropped a pill into his beer. She tossed a wink over her shoulder at me, then perched back on the stool next to her prey. My sister was a beautiful, sexy, black widow spider, cleverly constructing her web to the detriment of any man who got too close.

"Did she just slip him something?" Matt asked, his glass of tea halfway to his mouth.

"Um, did she?" I ducked my head.

"What are the two of you up to?" He clunked his glass on the table.

"Wait until you hear the information she has before you get angry. She has to get rid of him somehow, doesn't she? I don't want my sister dead like Jim."

"Dennis killed Jim?" Wayne asked.

"I think so. We just need the proof."

Matt scowled. "You leave that up to the authorities. You've done a good job digging up information, but there comes a point in any investigation when even the toughest cop has to call for backup."

"You're right. Once Dennis leaves, Angela will come over here, tell you what she found out, and we'll leave it all in your hands." I straightened as my food order arrived. The aroma of beef ribs basted in sauce tickled my senses. I practically drooled as I reached for the first bite. "Mary Ann and I will concentrate on who is harassing the shop owners. I don't think it's Dennis." I explained how someone had hired Phil and now that the pranks were continuing, that person was still working hard to run people off.

I lifted a rib to my mouth and took a bite. Barbecue sauce smeared my face. I could care less. "These are the most delicious things I've eaten in forever."

"Dennis just fell off his stool." Mary Ann tapped me on the shoulder.

I thought she'd been so wrapped up in whispering with Michael that she wasn't aware of what was going on around her. "Angela is calling him a cab. Good. That means he isn't dead."

"You thought she might kill him?"

Matt's eyes widened.

"Well, I hoped not, but drugs are iffy, aren't they?"

"I do not want to hear this." He dropped a rib bone on a plate set in the center of the table for such a purpose. "Yes, I do. Did your sister give Dennis Franklin an illegal drug?"

"I don't know what she gave him. She just said something to put him to sleep."

Matt jumped up from his chair, hard enough to send it crashing into the wall behind him. He rushed to where Dennis lay on the floor. Of course, I had to follow. I wasn't known as the nosiest of the Nelsons for nothing. Besides, despite what Angela might say, I was as guilty of anything that happened as she was.

"I just gave him an over the counter sleep aide," Angela said. "And no more than the required dosage. I don't want to go to prison, after all. Someone with my looks would never survive. It warns against taking with alcohol because it intensifies the sleepiness. He'll be fine."

Matt helped the extremely drowsy

man to his feet and outside to a waiting taxi. I grinned and high-fived my sister before leading her to our table where Wayne pulled up a chair.

"You two should really consider law enforcement," he said. "Undercover detectives. You make a good team."

Angela shook her head. "I could never work that close with Stormi. She likes to take charge of everything." She waved for the waitress, then ordered a salad. Big surprise. She held out her hand. "My fifty bucks, please."

While I waited for Matt to return, I paid her, then concentrated on my ribs. If I didn't keep my head down, I'd lose my appetite over the way Angela flirted with Wayne and Mary Ann hung on every word Michael said. Did I act that silly when Matt was with me? I shuddered and hoped I was a bit more sensible.

"He'll be fine," Matt said resuming his place at the table. "But, he wouldn't stop talking about the beautiful lady in red he was going to marry when he struck it rich."

Angela beamed. "My job here is

complete." She filled the men in on what transpired in her conversation with the drunk mailman. She sobered when she got to the fact that Ida was most likely in danger.

"We need to keep her from marrying the man," I said.

"You said you were going to leave it up to the authorities from now on," Matt said.

"Right. I did." Well, I could send the picture I'd taken with my cell phone to Ida. That wasn't overstepping any boundaries, right? Especially if I sent them anonymously.

Once we'd eaten, and the empty baskets removed from the table, Matt relaxed and ordered a beer. He rarely indulged, thankfully, so I had no problem with the occasional one.

"Do you know the two-step?" he asked.

I shook my head. "I'm not a very good dancer, although I do love to."

"I'll teach you." He pulled me onto the dance floor and into his arms.

The steps were simple to follow and

soon I was bending my knee and sliding across the floor with the rest of them. Maybe I should indulge in a pair of cowboy boots. Red ones. They'd be better for dancing than flip-flops and way more attractive.

Angela and Wayne glided past us, their bodies so close together no light could shine between them. I shook my head. They were completely out of step with everyone else.

"Don't worry," Matt told me. "He has a good head on his shoulders. I doubt he'll make baby daddy number three."

"I hope not. I'd like my sister to find a good man and settle down."

"Your mother and Robert Smithfield seem to be growing close. I spotted them having lunch at the park the other day. They were as cute as teenagers." He grinned. "But not as cute as us."

The song ended and went into a slow love song. Instead of heading back to the table, Matt pulled me closer and nestled my head into the crook of his shoulder. I could happily stay there forever.

The sound of glass breaking drew my

attention to the other side of the dance floor. A mere breath later, I found myself knocked on my back and staring at the ceiling from the man who had been thrown into me. Matt lunged forward and dove into the tussle.

I got to my feet and joined Mary Ann and Angela by the safety of the wall. "Why is it that I seem to get knocked down every time I'm on a date with Matt? It's either that or we get shot at."

"Maybe you need to step away from writing violent books," Angela said. "Erotica is safer and the research a lot more fun."

"Gross." I ducked as a chair hit the wall next to me. "That was almost as if they were trying to hit me." I would have sworn in court that the man looked straight at me before throwing the chair.

"It did come close," Mary Ann said.

I studied the crowd of punch-throwing, testosterone-induced men. While Matt, Wayne, and Michael did their best to break up the brawl, two muscular men with the glazed-eyed look of people deep into their drink, seemed to focus on the three of us against the wall. Me in particular.

If my hunch was correct, Matt wasn't going to want me investigating the pranks against the Main Street shop owners after tonight. I grabbed my sister's arm and Mary Ann's. "We've got to get out of here. The restroom."

We raced into the restroom and barricaded the door with the trashcan and our bodies. "Those men seem to be after me, don't you think?"

"Why?" Angela glowered. "You weren't doing anything but dancing. I was the one enticing Dennis."

"I don't think this has to do with Dennis." Someone shoved against the door. My feet slid. "Help me." They kicked off their shoes and planted their bare feet more firmly against the door.

"I'm calling Matt and telling him where we are," Mary Ann said. "They'll take care of those goons."

"You do know that if they start shooting, this thin wood won't stop a bullet," Angela pointed out.

"Thank you, Queen Obvious." I

pressed harder, opened my mouth, and did my best imitation of a girl about to be murdered.

Soon, the tiled restroom echoed with all three of our screams and the shoving against the door at our back stopped. We grinned at each other as Mary Ann's cell phone rang.

"It's Matt. He says to open the door."

I yanked it open and jumped aside, just in case one of those ginormous goons waited there. Instead, it was the shocked look of my beloved I came face-to-face with. He swiped a hand across his bloody lip.

"What is going on?"

"There were two men trying to kill me. Well, I don't know if they actually wanted to kill me, but they were definitely after me." I glanced up and down the hall. "I don't think someone wants me to find out who, and why, the shop owners are being bothered."

"The only way for someone to know you planned on continuing that path," he said, guiding me back to the main part of the bar, "is if that same someone followed you here and listened to our conversation over dinner."

22

It took a lot of guts to listen in on a conversation involving three law enforcement officers. Still, I agreed with Matt and kept glancing around us as he ushered me from the bar. As Matt helped me into his car, Wayne and Angela into hers, and Michael and Mary Ann climbed into mine, I saw the back of a man who looked suspiciously like Thomas. Still, I couldn't help but feel as if we were being ushered home because we'd broken a rule of some sort.

We congregated at my place, filling the small kitchen, and eventually spilling into the backyard. Mom and Robert arrived a few minutes after we did, and Mom rushed to make lemonade and tea.

While I still wasn't sure how much Robert knew about what I went through to write an interesting mystery, I assumed Mom told him everything. Hopefully, the banker could be trusted.

"I'll be calling Dennis Franklin and Steve Larkin into the precinct for more questioning," Matt said. "As the only two people who might have a grievance against you, they're the most likely to have hired muscle to threaten you."

"Don't forget Mrs. Rogers." I stretched out in a lawnchair.

"I'm serious."

"I know. Do you think the fight at the bar was a ruse to get you away from me?"

"Yes. But, I also think that if someone wanted you dead, you would be. I think those two strangers were only meant to intimidate, not physically harm. With all three of us men away from you, it wouldn't have been hard to kill you."

"Since you officers are here," Robert said, stepping out of the kitchen, "I'd like to file a complaint. If you want me to go in the morning to make a formal statement, I will. It seems the bank, and other shops, have a sudden infestation of rats." He speared me a glance. "You need to get to the bottom of this. It won't take long for the rodents to gain access to the bakery."

I put a hand to my chest. "Why are you looking at me?"

"It doesn't appear as if you've done anything with the information I gave you."

"She told me," Matt said. "All it did was make Steve Larkin a person of interest. Having a lot of money in the bank doesn't mean the man is committing a crime or intends to commit one."

Robert shrugged. "Perhaps, but it isn't Dennis Franklin that I see skulking around town. It's Larkin's man, Thomas."

"I'm hearing that from several people." Matt planted a kiss on my forehead. "I'll see you in the morning. Again, don't go anywhere alone, and make sure you at least have your Tazer."

"I will."

The men left, leaving us women to sort through the details alone.

"I wish I would have been at Roy's,"

Mom said. "I love a good honky-tonk fight."

"You should have seen Angela. She deserves an academy award for the way she came on to Dennis."

Angela blew on her nails and wiped them on her shirt. "I was amazing, wasn't I?" She grinned. "It wasn't easy. The man smells of body odor. I have no idea what Ida sees in him."

Which reminded me I needed to have some photos delivered to the widow in the morning. I'd make sure Angela's face wasn't recognizable. I appreciated my sister's help and didn't want to repay her by putting her in danger. I'd been there done that.

"I'm ready for bed. It's been a long day." I pushed to my feet.

"I'll be over in the morning," Mary Ann said, walking with me into the house. "What's on the agenda?"

"Delivering cheating photos to Ida, then spying on Larkin, I guess. Maybe follow Dennis around a bit. I feel like we've run up against a brick wall again."

"What does your gut tell you?"

"That Dennis is the killer. I just don't know how to prove it." Unless I accused him face-to-face, which it might come down to. I'd wait until after Matt questioned him in the morning. "He's the one with the most to gain over Jim's death."

"What about Phil?"

"I think he got in the way." I walked her to the front door and watched as she headed down the sidewalk toward the house she shared with Matt.

Across the street, Mrs. Rogers's curtains fluttered into place. From the opposite direction, my neighbors, the Salazars, waved as they entered their house. A moment of guilt over them taking over most of the Neighborhood Watch responsibilities washed over me. Maybe I could give them a potted plant as a thank you gift. In yet another direction, Rusty meandered toward his house. He dragged what looked like the handle to a shovel. The sound was so much like bony fingers scratching against the floor that I shuddered.

I waved and went inside. Mom and

Angela had already gone to their rooms, leaving me to turn off the lights and close the house up for the night.

In bed, I stared at the ceiling and did something I rarely allowed. I called for my cats, Ebony and Ivory, and Sadie to all crawl in bed with me. Sadie lay her massive head across my legs and let out a contented sigh. I reached down and played with her ears as my brain whirled in an effort to find something solid to take to Matt in regards to Dennis.

I had nothing other than a feeling deep in my gut that I had learned not to ignore. If Matt didn't find the evidence he needed during his interrogation tomorrow, I would have to instigate a violent reaction from Dennis.

Thankfully, I fell asleep by midnight and got seven hours of sleep before Sadie nudged me to the fact she needed to go out. I padded to the kitchen, let her out, then shuffled to my office where I printed out the photos of Cheating Dennis. I located an empty manila envelope and slid the pictures inside. Now to figure out a way of putting them where she was bound to see them and Dennis couldn't find them first.

"Put the envelope between her door and the screen door," Mary Ann said when I asked her an hour later. "Then, make an anonymous phone call letting her know the pictures are there. Dennis will be busy at the station for an hour or two. If we go to Ida's now, we should be able to leave the photos and get out without being discovered."

"Good plan." I'd skip my morning coffee until we made the drop off. But, there was no way I could spy on Steve Larkin without caffeine.

We pulled in front of a house a few doors down from Ida's and ran at a crouch to her front porch. While I headed behind a bush and dialed her phone number, Mary Ann slipped the envelope between the door and the screen, rang the doorbell, and leaped behind the bush with me.

"A package has been delivered," I said, making my voice as hoarse as possible when Ida answered.

Seconds later, the front door opened.

Ida stepped out, glanced around, then noticed the envelope. She opened it, cursed, and marched inside, leaving the screen to slam closed behind her.

First job of the day, check. I high-fived Mary Ann and ran for the car. Once inside, I texted Matt, who told me that Dennis had a rock solid alibi for the night of Jim's murder. "Let me guess," I said, showing Mary Ann the text, "his alibi is Ida."

"I don't think she'll cover for him anymore." She grinned. "I also don't think she'll change her story, because it might implicate her, but it won't hurt to let Matt know so he can question her again. Let's head to the station. Have I mentioned how much I love being your assistant?"

"Wait until I actually have a license. We'll really have fun, then."

As we pulled in front of the police station, Steve Larkin was getting out of his car. He glanced our way and frowned.

"Can this day get any worse?" He asked.

"I'm sure it can." I returned his frown

with a smile. "Let's see if I can help." I crossed my arms and blocked the entrance to the station. "A couple of thugs tried to kill me last night. You wouldn't happen to know anything about that, now, would you?"

"This is ridiculous. I've given up on this insane town." He leaned against the hand rail. "No amount of money is worth this trouble."

"So you do know about it."

"They were only hired to scare you into backing off, not hurt you. You are the most tenacious woman I've ever met. Next to you, is the beautiful Norma, who I gather only agreed to go out with me in order to gather information for you." He closed his eyes and exhaled sharply. "Look, Miss Nelson. I admire a woman with your spirit. I'm not going to admit to hiring Phil Davidson or anyone else to terrorize the shopowners. I'm going to answer a few questions for Detective Steele and leave town. Will that make you happy?"

I thrust out my hand. "Very happy, Mr. Larkin. I wish you luck. Maybe you can build that mall in Harrisburg. The citizens are a little more sane over there."

"I will take that into consideration." He gave me a pained smile and entered the precinct.

One down, one to go. Dennis Franklin was going to be a tougher egg to crack.

Mary Ann and I followed Steve into the building. While he was led to a back room by Wayne, we approached Angela at the reception desk.

"I have to tell you," she said. "Dennis was not happy to see me sitting here."

"Is he still being interviewed?" I asked.

"No, he left about fifteen minutes ago. After giving me the third degree about whether I worked for the police in an official," she made quotes for official, "capacity, he got a phone call that made his face turn red, and dashed out of here like his plump rear end was on fire." She shook her head. "He promised to call me tonight."

"You gave him your phone number?" I thought she was smarter than that.

"Of course." She gave an evil grin. "I told him to call 871-5673."

I peered over her desk at the phone and tried to decipher the message. "You called him a loser?"

She shrugged one pink silk-covered shoulder. "He won't know that. He'll only know there is no such number. The guy is weird. I can't be caught alone with him."

I agreed. If she was, and he found out she was playing him, my sister might be the next person whose head got shoved into a vat of chocolate. Or worse. Almost any way of dying would be worse in my opinion.

I leaned on her desk. "I need you to do something for me."

"More? Haven't I done enough?" She rolled her eyes.

"Do you have his number?"

She nodded.

"I want you to text him and ask him to meet you at the park tonight at seven o'clock." I held up a hand to ward off her protest. "I'll be the one actually meeting him."

"Not alone!"

Aww. My big sister did care about me. "Have you seen the park in the summer? It's crowded. I won't be alone."

"That's right," Mom said, stepping up behind us. "I knew you two were up to something dangerous, so I followed you. I'll be hiding in the bushes tonight with my cell phone ready to dial 911."

23

"Aunt Stormi?" Dakota hovered in the doorway of my bedroom.

I turned from the mirror. My hair was in a ponytail and out of my face. I had on my running shoes, just in case, and wore my most comfortable Capri yoga pants. If things turned nasty, I was pretty confident I could outrun Dennis. "What's up?"

"I thought you could use these." He opened his hand. "Earpieces. One for you and one for your sidekick. Grandma, I guess. They'll be able to hear everything that goes on."

"This is wonderful." I slipped the earpiece over my ear and removed the hair tie from my hair. I could bear the heat of long hair if it meant my safety.

"Thank you."

"I'll be in the house with a tape recorder," he said. "We'll get everything that happens on tape. That should give us all the evidence we need to convict Mr. Franklin."

I clapped him on the shoulder. "You, my dear, are an excellent detective."

"Remember that when I'm eighteen and we go into business together," he said, walking beside me.

"I don't think I'll ever stop writing books, Dakota. My private investigator license is to help me do that."

"You never know what the future holds. I have two years for you to change your mind."

He did indeed. Right now, I had something else entirely that needed my full attention.

Mom, dressed all in black as she always insisted on doing when we ventured out at night, paced the kitchen floor. Angela sat at the table, drumming her fingers, and staring at what looked like recording equipment.

"Mom, you do realize it won't be

dark for another two hours, right?" I grabbed a couple of water bottles from the fridge. "Not to mention, you're going to swelter in that get-up."

"I can't be seen. That will ruin the entire plan."

I rolled my eyes and grabbed a small backpack I used on the rare occasions I went hiking. I tossed in the water, my gun, my Tazer, and two granola bars. It never hurt to be prepared.

"All you have to do is push the little button on the back of the device," Dakota instructed. "Don't forget. If you don't press it, we can't hear you, and you'll be out there alone."

"Not alone." Mom held up a finger. "I'm there."

"You're wearing one, too." He handed Mom an earpiece and pulled the beanie off her head. "You have to cover it with your hair."

"But my hair shines in the moonlight." She patted her blond strands.

"It isn't dark yet." I slung the backpack over my shoulder. "Let's go." I pressed the button so I wouldn't forget and rushed out the front door.

I had fifteen minutes to get to the assigned bench by the fountain. Once Dennis showed up and realized he'd been tricked, I expected to have to do some fast talking to keep him from getting physical. If he was Jim's and Phil's killer, as I suspected, he wouldn't hesitate to kill again. I'd be the one in his line of fire.

"I'm trusting you to call Matt right away if something goes wrong," I said to Mom as we got into the car.

"Don't worry. I'll call him and every other law enforcement officer I can get on the line."

I was counting on it. I had texted Matt where I was going but hadn't heard back. It was for the best. He'd only try to convince me not to go.

I parked as close to the designated spot as I deemed safe. "Show time." I glanced at my watch. I had five minutes to get to the bench. "I don't know how much he will be able to hear if you start talking, so talk softly, okay?"

Mom nodded. "I'll be behind those

thick bushes over there. I'll be able to see, and hear, everything."

I nodded and, clutching my backpack like a lifeline, made my way to the carved concrete bench and perched on the edge. The five foot fountain, depicting frolicking dolphins, bubbled away. Children screamed and laughed from nearby play equipment. It was the safest and most crowded section of the park.

The early evening sun warmed my shoulders, and despite a slight breeze, a fine sheen of perspiration appeared on my upper lip. Arkansas summer humidity at its finest. I slapped at a mosquito and waited. And waited. And waited.

By seven thirty, I knew Dennis was a no-show.

"Where is he?" Mom's voice came through my earpiece.

"Not here." I stood and arched my back to get the kinks out. "Sorry, Dakota. You recorded a half hour of nothing."

"Better than recording your death," he said.

True. Very, very true.

Mom joined me. "Let's take a drive

through town. If we're lucky enough to spot him, we can come up with another plan."

"Makes as much sense as anything." We'd come that far, and I didn't want to return home without accomplishing my mission.

"Don't do anything stupid," Dakota said through the earpiece. "Matt and Wayne are here at the house listening to everything you do."

"Thanks for the warning." I grinned.

My man was never far away when I put myself into a dangerous situation. If he could tie me up to keep me safe, he would. Unfortunately, he knew that would put a very large wedge between us. As long as I didn't break the law, which I did my best not to do anymore, he let me do my thing.

I drove down Main Street as slowly as possible, only speeding up if an impatient driver got behind me. "We should park and walk."

"I agree. Your driving is making me nuts."

"I'm only trying to see between the

buildings." I pulled into a vacant spot in front of the drugstore. "If I go too fast, we might miss him."

Mom shoved open her door. "We don't even know if he's here."

Maybe not, but a Mrs. Rogers walking at the pace of a speedwalker and looking over her shoulder might be just as good as finding Dennis Franklin. I shoved open my door and hurried to catch up with her.

"Mrs. Rogers. Wait." Thankful for my gym shoes, I jogged to her side. "Are you all right?"

"Go away. I need to get home."

"My mother and I can give you a ride. We're here to locate Dennis Franklin, but—"

She grabbed my arm and yanked me between the bank and an empty storefront. "You don't want to mess with that man." She wagged her finger in my face. "I know you're nosy and like to stick your nose into things that don't concern you, but that man is—" She glanced over my shoulder and paled.

I turned to see a plump man wearing

a ski mask and lime green sneakers aiming a gun at us. And, in typical fashion, I'd left my backpack, which contained my gun and Tazer, in the car with Mom.

The gunman motioned for Mrs. Rogers and I to proceed down the alley and into a blue panel van. At first, I thought maybe the two of us could overpower him and take his gun, but Mrs. Rogers shook like an old Chihuahua and the papers, more fliers to run me out of town, rattled in her hands like skeletal bones. Our only chance to stay alive at this point was to cooperate.

I put my hand on her elbow and helped her into the van. The gunman yanked the fliers from her hand and tossed them toward a dumpster. They fluttered to the ground and away from us like fuschia-colored leaves.

"Get in," he ordered.

I climbed in the back. "Where are we going?"

"Shut up." He slammed the door, casting us into darkness. Seconds later, the van roared to life and we headed to only God knew where.

"Aunt Stormi?" Dakota's whisper reminded me I had more company than just an old lady who disliked me.

"Yes."

"Where are you?"

"In the back of a van. I'm pretty sure my abductor is Dennis Franklin. He's wearing lime green gym shoes and driving a blue panel van. Mrs. Rogers is with me."

"Who are you talking to?" Mrs. Rogers peered through the gloom at my face. "Or are you so touched in the head that you're talking to yourself?"

I moved my hair and showed her the earpiece. "You are now part of a sting operation, Mrs. Rogers. Hush."

"I'm following the van," Mom said. "It turned onto Highway 64."

"Stormi?" Matt's voice brought tears to my eyes. "Do whatever you have to, but do not, I repeat, do not, provoke him."

"I'll do my best, but if he lays hands on me…"

Dennis banged on the wall. "No

talking!"

"I'm telling your mother, Dennis Franklin." Mrs. Rogers shouted back. "I don't care if she is in a nursing home. She deserves to know what a low-down snake her son is."

The van swerved and came to a stop sudden enough to dump us onto the floor. "Please, stop, Mrs. Rogers. We don't want to die tonight." I got to my hands and knees, ready to fight if need be.

The back of the van opened. Dennis reached in, hit Mrs. Rogers in the head with a two-foot board, knocking her unconscious, then climbed back out. "I said no talking. Stupid women who don't listen." He slammed the door closed again.

I scrambled to the old woman's side and felt for a pulse. Steady, but weak. "He hit Mrs. Rogers, but she's still alive. I have to stop talking."

"Then just listen," Matt said. "Is there anything you can use as a weapon? One grunt for yes, two for no."

The van started moving again, making my own movements clumsy. I crawled around the back of the van, encountering nothing more than empty food wrappers. I grunted twice.

"I'm right behind the van," Mom said. "The next time Dennis gets out, I'll hit him with the car."

"Do not do that, Anne," Matt told her.

My mother was going to get me killed. I scooted until my back was against the side of the van. I was weaponless with no food or water and at the mercy of a madman. I tried to think of where he could possibly be taking me.

"I think someone needs to contact Ida and make sure she's all right. If she broke things off with Dennis, he could be a bit deranged." I kept my voice as low as possible.

The van slowed, finally coming to a stop. A shot rang out. Mom screamed.

I bolted to my feet and banged against the van door. "Let me out! He fired a shot, Matt. He's trying to kill my mother."

"Hush, Stormi," Matt said. "He just called us asking for five hundred thousand dollars ransom for you.

Cooperate. You're more valuable to him alive."

The van doors opened and I fell to the ground. Rocks dug into my hands and knees.

Dennis wrapped his fist into my hair and yanked me to my feet. He ripped the earpiece from my ear and bashed it with the butt of his gun. "Now, get over there with your nosy mother."

I was so relieved to see that he had only shot out the tire on my car that I sagged against the Mercedes. Mom wrapped her arms around me. "I still have my earpiece," she whispered.

I nodded and watched as he dragged Mrs. Rogers from the van. Her head bounced against the fender, then the ground.

"Mrs. Rogers needs medical attention," I said loud enough, I hoped, to be heard through Mom's earpiece.

"Stupid woman. She can lay there and rot." He laughed. "After all, where's she going to go?" He motioned for Mom and I to move ahead of him. "I have the perfect little cabin to stash you two in," he said. "Maybe I'll up the ransom to include your mother. A bestselling author such as Stormi Nelson should have enough money in her account. If not, I'm sure the bakery will bring in enough funds for me to live quite nicely in Barbados."

"What did you do with Ida?" I asked.

24

"I didn't do anything with that nagging harpy." He unlocked the front door on a ramshackle cabin. "Watch your step. These boards are rotting. You won't bring me any money dead."

That's a relief. At least he didn't intend on killing us, at least not right away. I took Mom's arm and steered her around a hole in the porch floor. Behind us, Mrs. Rogers twitched. Thank you, God, she was still breathing. Hopefully, she would gain consciousness in time to help us.

"Sit over there." Dennis waved us toward a sofa so stained the original color was indistinguishable and stuffing was visible through several holes. "I don't want to tie you two up, but I will if I have to. I'm not a fan of violence against

290

women.”

“Tell that to Mrs. Rogers,” I muttered.

“That couldn’t be helped.” He scowled. “I have a bad back. There was no way I could lift her and lower her gently to the ground.”

“The obvious reason for killing Jim Worthington was for his money,” I said, glancing out the window in hopes Mrs. Rogers had moved. She hadn’t. “But why put him in the bakery?”

“I couldn’t leave him in the alley.” Dennis shook his head and glanced at his watch. “I needed time to establish my alibi. A smart sleuth such as yourself should know that.”

“I guess it messed up your plans that shop owners weren’t willing to sell out.”

Why couldn’t Mom sit still? She moved around next to me like a child who needed to go potty.

“Yes, but there are other ways to achieve the same means. When Ida found out I liked the ladies a bit too much, she kicked me out. Won’t even share her husband’s life insurance.” He shook his head as if the thought was completely alien to him. "We had a deal, her and I. If she came into a lot of money, we would get married and go away together."

"Then, you would kill her."

"No! I love her, as much as I'm able to love just one woman."

"Does she know you killed her husband?"

"I don't think so." He frowned at Mom. "Why do you keep fidgeting?"

"I need to use the restroom."

"I doubt it works, but it's through that door."

She dashed into the room and slammed the door.

"Did you kill Phil?" I asked.

He shrugged. "The nosy little twerp saw something he shouldn't. Didn't his mother ever tell him that painting graffiti on public property would get him in trouble?"

Mom raced past the cabin window. My mouth fell open. She left me. My mother left me alone with a madman. She stooped beside Mrs. Rogers, glanced around, and sprinted down the dirt road away from the cabin.

"Oh, well." Dennis shrugged. "I'll be gone before she can get help. You're the one worth the real money."

"You do know that just because I'm an author doesn't make me rich, right?" Such a common misconception. I've done all right for myself, and have no complaints, but I'm no Janet Evanovich or Stephen King.

"I read a magazine article on you when you made your first million dollars." He waved the gun at me. "So, don't pretend you don't have any money. I only want half."

He pulled up a rickety wooden chair, sat down, and stared at me. "You're quite lovely. You wouldn't contemplate coming to the tropics with me, would you?"

I shook my head. "I prefer a more solid, trustworthy type of man, but thanks for the offer." Like Matt. Where was my mother?

"Oh, look," he said, glancing out the window. "Mrs. Rogers is gone. That's good. I was wondering how I was going to back the van out of the yard with her body in the way." Another look at his watch and we were leaving the cabin and heading for the van.

"Are we heading for the ransom drop?" I reached for the van doorhandle.

"You may sit up front." He shook his head. "I can't take you with me, dear. I'll leave you in a secure location and tell the police where to find you once I am long gone."

"Why not here?"

"I want to be out of the country before your mother leads them here. My best chance of that is to leave you somewhere else." He tapped the barrel of the pistol against his head. "I have a backup plan."

"Did you plan for this?" Mrs. Rogers hit him across the side of the head with the very board he had knocked her out with.

He crumbled to the ground like a balloon that had suddenly lost its air. The gun slid under the van.

"I hope you have something to tie him up with," she said, handing me my purse. "I got this out of the van. I'm feeling nauseous." She turned away and lost her dinner in the dirt.

I crawled under the van and retrieved the gun. "Help me drag him to the cabin."

"Just lock him in the back of the van." She leaned against the vehicle. "We can drive back to town."

"Duh." I fished the keys from his front pocket and, with Mrs. Rogers's help, hoisted him into the back of the van.

Leaving her to climb into the front seat, I raced for the cabin and searched until I found a length of rope. Back at the van, I tied Dennis's hands and feet together, locked the back of the van and slid behind the steering wheel.

I grinned at Mrs. Rogers. "Thanks."

"No problem." She waved a hand in my direction, keeping her eyes closed. "Drive carefully, please. I do believe I have a concussion."

I started the van and steered it down the dirt road. Night had fallen and that far out in the country it got very dark. I turned on the van lights and illuminated my mother on the side of the road. She was bent over at the waist, struggling for breath.

She held up a thumb like a hitchhiker. "Thank the good Lord. I need to exercise more. I was never going to make it to town and had no idea how to tell Matthew where we are. Yes, Matthew, I have Stormi. Her and Mrs. Rogers are now driving the van. I don't know where Dennis is." She raised her eyebrows at me.

"In the back."

"He's in the back of the van. We're headed to town. Meet us at the station." Mom squeezed in beside Mrs. Rogers. "Do you know how to get back to town?"

"I have no idea, but we do have GPS on my phone." I went through the directory, found my home address, and set the phone on the dashboard.

"This was the easiest escape we've ever had," Mom said. "We're getting better at this solving crime thing. Thanks to Dakota, the police now have Mr. Franklin's confession. This case is signed, sealed, and delivered."

I reached across Mrs. Rogers and grabbed her hand. "You're the best sidekick a girl could want."

"We do make a good team." Mom squeezed my hand in return. "How did you get away?"

"I rescued her," Mrs. Rogers said, opening one eye. "But that doesn't mean I like her. I'm still going to try and get her run out of town."

"Duly noted." I laughed. I, quite possibly, owed the woman my life. She could put up as many fliers about me as she wanted.

"What do you have against my daughter?" Uh-oh. I recognized the Mama Bear look in Mom's eyes.

"She's a romance writer."

"So?"

Mrs. Rogers sighed. "Romance novels ruined my marriage."

"You've got to do better than that," Mom said.

"I'm injured."

"You don't know injured. Injured is what I'll do to you unless you have a good reason for bullying my kid."

"Fine. I was so involved in reading about fictional romances, that I ruined my own." A tear slid down her wrinkled cheek. "I compared my Horace to the heroes in the novels. The house was dirty, dinner was either late or burned, until the poor man couldn't take it anymore. I swore then and there not to open another romance novel."

I cocked my head. "Just because you don't read them, doesn't mean a lot of other people don't. Besides, my books are romantic true-crime mysteries. That's a little different."

"That's right," Mom said, with a nod. "She'll be writing about this fiasco with Dennis. You're a hero, Mrs. Rogers."

She made a sound deep in her throat. "I'll think about it."

"Ask Matt to meet us at the hospital," I said. "I don't like Mrs. Rogers's color."

"Now, you're criticizing my looks?" She opened both eyes. "I'll have you no that I was quite the beauty in my day."

"You look a bit pale. I think you need to see a doctor."

"Fine."

Two hours later I pulled up to the emergency entrance of the Oak Meadows Hospital. Matt and Wayne met us at the door and helped Mrs. Rogers to a wheelchair.

"I'll go with her," Wayne offered. "You deal with your girl."

"Gladly." Matt grinned and wrapped me in his arms. "That was close." He pulled back and rested his forehead against mine. "Are you finished scaring me by going on these wild adventures?"

I laughed. "Oh, honey, I'm just getting started. Remember," I said, tapping his nose with my finger. "I'm getting my investigator's license."

He groaned and lowered his head to kiss me.

Camera flashes and shouted questions from Nancy Rhino surrounded us. What other girl in Oak Meadows received such a homecoming?

The End

Enjoy other mysteries by Cynthia
Hickey

Nosy Neighbor Series
Anything For A Mystery, **Book 1**
A Killer Plot, **Book 2**
Skin Care Can Be Murder, **Book 3**

The Summer Meadows Series
Fudge-Laced Felonies, **Book 1**
Candy-Coated Secrets, **Book 2**
Chocolate-Covered Crime, **Book 3**
Maui Macadamia Madness, **Book 4**
All four novels in one collection

The River Valley Mystery Series
Deadly Neighbors, **Book 1**
Advance Notice, **Book 2**
The Librarian's Last Chapter, **Book 3**
All three novels in one collection

See Cynthia's other books at
www.cynthiahickey.com

ABOUT THE AUTHOR

www.cynthiahickey.com

Cynthia Hickey is a multi-published and best-selling author of cozy mysteries and romantic suspense. She has taught writing at many conferences and small writing retreats. She and her husband run the publishing press, Winged Publications. They live in Arizona and Arkansas, becoming snowbirds with three dogs. They have ten grandchildren who keep them busy and tell everyone they know that "Nana is a writer."

Connect with me on FaceBook
Twitter
Sign up for my newsletter and receive a free short story
www.cynthiahickey.com

Follow me on Amazon
And Bookbub
Shop my bookstore here. For better
price and autographed.

www.ingramcontent.com/pod-product-compliance
Lightning Source LLC
Chambersburg PA
CBHW061014120726
47910CB00006B/1930